SHERLOCK HOLMES
AND THE
MYCROFT INCIDENT

The Early Casebook of Sherlock Holmes

Book Seven

Linda Stratmann

SAPERE
BOOKS

SHERLOCK HOLMES
AND THE
MYCROFT INCIDENT

Published by Sapere Books.

24 Trafalgar Road, Ilkley, LS29 8HH
United Kingdom

saperebooks.com

ISBN: 978-0-85495-345-5

From
Memoirs of a Medical Man
by A. Stamford FRCS

1924

CHAPTER ONE

Sherlock Holmes acquired many secrets throughout his long and illustrious career. Some of these were so sensitive and dangerous that he was precluded from sharing them even with his closest and most trusted associate, Dr John Watson. Lives were at stake, and the security of our greatest institutions, even the nation itself, hung in the balance. There was one secret, however, which cut close to his innermost self. The year was 1877, and as it chanced, I became involved, both as a fellow student and as Holmes's friend. Some secrets can lose their power over time, and it is only now, with that assurance and Holmes's permission, that I can share an account of what occurred. He never discussed the events with me again, and even when out of necessity he made some passing allusion to the disturbing and tragic circumstances, he would refer to them only as 'the incident'.

The autumn term at Barts had just commenced. I had returned to London following a short sojourn in Paris with my friend, classics scholar George Luckhurst. Together we savoured the elevated delights of the museums of art, which was followed, at my special request, by a tour of the catacombs with the famous ossuary. Luckhurst was only able to recover from the horrors of this latter visit by plunging into the dazzling splendour of the Grands Magasins for some restorative shopping.

I had not seen Sherlock Holmes for some while and when he did not appear at the laboratory, I decided to pay a call on him at his rooms in Montague Street. Those of my readers who are familiar with Dr John Watson's memoirs will have been amused by his descriptions of the apparently chaotically arranged interior of the apartment they later shared in Baker Street. I can assure you; this was as nothing compared to Montague Street, which was just as cluttered but also far smaller and less luxurious. His landlady, who was not cast from that redoubtable mould which produced Mrs Hudson, was disinclined to do other than the bare minimum required. That day, I recall, she was distracted from her duties by the arrival of a niece with a new baby to admire.

When I made my way up to Holmes's room, I found him in the throes of applying some method to his collection of newspaper cuttings, having purchased a new commonplace book, since the earlier one was overfilled and bulging. The piles of newspapers in Holmes's room had by now assumed the appearance of a range of craggy mountains, but were, so Holmes assured me, in a state of the most perfect order and which were not under any circumstances to be disturbed except under his direction. He greeted me briefly and soon had me busy assisting him with scissors and paste, commenting from time to time on the articles which had attracted his interest.

He was not smoking his pipe at the time, probably due to the not inconsiderable risk of conflagration, though the air in the room was as ever thick with the smell of tobacco. I did think of asking for coffee to be sent up, but rather doubted that it would appear, or be drinkable if it did.

'I wonder,' he said, holding up a page of small notices, 'if Mr Anthony Cloudsdale has reappeared? His family has paid for the usual two lines asking for him or anyone who has seen him, to get in touch with them. What strange story lies beneath that anxious appeal?'

'Do you know that gentleman?' I asked.

'No, although my brother has mentioned his name in passing.'

It took a moment or two for me to appreciate the important part of that statement. 'I didn't know you had a brother,' I said. 'Is he older or younger?'

'Mycroft is seven years my senior,' said Holmes.

I was eager to know more, and struggled to light on a question which would not appear to be prying or impertinent. Holmes recognised my dilemma, and with a wry smile continued. 'He has his own small circle of friends but is mainly to be found at his office in Whitehall, where he has a minor post as a government accountant. He dines at his club, and his preferred exercise is a solitary walk about St James's Park. We see each other occasionally.'

That appeared to be all Holmes wished to say on the subject, and we continued our work, interrupted only by the sound of a smart double rap at the front door. 'That will be him now,' he said.

'Do you have an appointment?' I asked. 'I had better go.'

'There is no appointment, and you are welcome to stay.'

Eleven years were to pass before Holmes so much as mentioned to John Watson that he had a brother, and he and Watson had then been friends since 1881, the year in which I introduced them. I feel sure that Holmes must eventually have told Watson something of what had previously transpired, but only on the understanding that he did not record it in his memoirs. The Mycroft Holmes whom Watson met was reclusive and corpulent, largely inactive apart from the application of a brilliant mind. The brother I met was only a possibility of what he would later become. I sometimes think that had things turned out differently, he might have had another future.

It is often the case that siblings will be unalike, one more closely resembling the mother, the other a likeness of the father, and so it was with Sherlock and Mycroft. Sherlock at twenty-three still retained a trace of boyishness in his appearance, which he soon shed as he approached his prime, becoming lean and spare with a wiry strength and intense, hard features. Mycroft, at the age of thirty, was more rounded of face, with a naturally amiable expression, broad of figure, and fleshy, but with a hint of potential power in his form.

'I see your housekeeper was late with the shaving water this morning,' said Mycroft, as Holmes introduced us. 'Mr Stamford, delighted to make your acquaintance, I hope you enjoyed your recent stay in Paris. I have never been there, but I understand the Rue de Rivoli is delightful in the autumn.'

I must have looked astonished, for he smiled and said, 'I doubt that you habitually carry a guide to the Louvre in your pocket. And no English barber would or could have cut your hair so — à la mode.'

Holmes ruefully rubbed his chin. 'I assume you have come to discuss Mr Cloudsdale,' he said, moving a pile of newspapers from a chair so Mycroft could be seated. 'Do you have further news of him? Stamford is trustworthy and I would like him to remain,' Holmes added, as Mycroft glanced questioningly at me.

Mycroft made himself comfortable, and the brothers, both now at their ease, faced each other. I sensed, not precisely affection, but a strong mutual trust, an unbreakable bond.

'There is no news, and the matter is more serious than any newspaper is aware of,' said Mycroft. 'Cloudsdale is aged forty-five and has been a trusted government servant for many years. He enjoys the highest level of approval and has access to documents which most men are not permitted to see. He has also on many occasions acted as a courier, transporting papers of the utmost importance and secrecy, which are required to be delivered by hand. Three weeks ago on the Monday morning, he departed the office with a sealed packet of papers which was secured in a special pocket in his clothing. I do not know what the papers were or where he was taking them. I am not supposed to know. His mission should have been completed in time for him to return to his duties later that day. He did not return and has not been seen since.'

'And the papers?' asked Holmes. 'Have they disappeared?'

'No. They were delivered safely. It was only after doing so that he vanished.'

'I assume the police have made the usual enquiries?'

'They have, without result. There are several theories. He may have suffered an accident or been taken ill. He might have been the victim of a common street robbery. He might have been waylaid and either kidnapped or killed by foreign agents for the papers his assailants thought he still carried. He may, and this is an especially distressing suggestion, have been selling secrets to another government, and has voluntarily gone into hiding.'

Holmes nodded thoughtfully at each of these theories. 'How well do you know Mr Cloudsdale?' he asked.

'I have only spoken to him occasionally on professional subjects. However, his poor wife who is understandably distressed, frequently comes to the office asking if we have learned anything. She goes to sit in the waiting room, and one of us is assigned to talk to her, but we have nothing to say except words of comfort. There are three children, the eldest son is at the University of Cambridge, the younger is said to be a good scholar and there is a daughter soon to be launched upon society. I am told she has both brains and beauty which is a fearsome combination.'

'As you say there may be a simple explanation, although the circumstances are suggestive,' said Holmes.

'I have, however, recently learned through certain channels of information of an additional factor which I will only reveal to you under terms of the strictest secrecy,' said Mycroft. He glanced at me once more.

'Proceed,' said Holmes.

'When Cloudsdale arrived at his destination, he was later than expected. He also appeared not to be his normal self. He was troubled, and unsettled in some way, and when asked if he was well, or had experienced any difficulty on the journey, he said only that there had been an unexpected delay on his route. He handed over the papers in their sealed envelope and departed. Usually the recipient of the envelope, a senior manager of long service who I am told is entirely trustworthy, would have unsealed it privately and extracted the contents, but Mr Cloudsdale's unusual demeanour made him hesitate. He decided to subject the envelope to a close examination, first by eye and then using a magnifying glass. When he did so, he detected signs which suggested that the envelope had been very expertly unsealed and resealed. Had he unsealed the envelope in the usual way, the evidence of tampering would have been destroyed. He called upon special assistance to open the envelope and to serve as witnesses to the process, and the papers were extracted. They did not appear to have been tampered with, but an expert analyst thought that they had been unfolded and laid out flat, presumably to be examined, and then folded again.'

'How late was Cloudsdale's arrival?' asked Holmes. 'Was there time for the papers to have been copied?'

'Less than thirty minutes,' said Mycroft. 'Not nearly long enough. I have been told that there were three documents, two written, one with a detailed plan. And enquiries have confirmed that there were no unusual transport delays that day, either by road or rail. Cloudsdale must have broken his journey somewhere, but we don't yet know where, or how that time was employed.'

'The date?' asked Holmes with a quizzical look, as he began to inspect a pile of newspapers.

Mycroft smiled knowingly. 'The weather that day was dull and overcast with heavy cloud and showers of rain,' he said. 'Photography would have taken far too long, even if it were possible.'

Holmes ceased his search. 'Go on,' he said.

'Naturally the office was alerted by telegram. It was decided not to alarm Cloudsdale on his arrival but allow him to be admitted to his desk in the usual way, then quietly conducted to a private room for interview. But he did not return. Enquiries were made at his home, but his wife had not seen him since his departure for work that morning. In view of the tampering with the papers, the police are treating his disappearance as highly significant.'

There was a moment of silence as we digested this. Naturally I felt considerable sympathy for Mrs Cloudsdale in her plight, but I could not see how even Holmes could match the resources of an entire police force in the search for a missing man.

'And perhaps, Mycroft,' said Holmes, with a keenly enquiring look, 'you could now elaborate on precisely what has brought you here?'

'Ah, yes,' sighed Mycroft. 'You must recall Joshua Emmett?'

'I do.'

Mycroft turned to me in explanation. 'Emmett and I were at school together. I have known him for twenty years. He is probably my closest friend. A good, honest fellow, trustworthy and a hard worker. He is a clerk in government service although not in my department. Not of the first ranking of intellect, but reliable. He recently became engaged to be married to a most charming young lady, a Miss Jessup. Since Cloudsdale's disappearance all those who knew him even slightly, and that includes Emmett, have been carefully questioned. Everyone employed at the Whitehall offices was either at his post or did not have an unexplained absence that day, but it is feared that one of his colleagues might have been in some way involved. Although the police will not say if they have any suspects, it is obvious to me that they are devoting more than the usual attention to Emmett. Not that they have any reason to suspect him of involvement, it is only that his recent engagement and marriage plans suggest that he was anticipating a substantial expense, and Miss Jessup is not in possession of a fortune. In their minds, he was vulnerable to bribery and blackmail.'

'What is your opinion?' I asked.

'A more open and straightforward man does not exist,' said Mycroft. 'I am sorry to say that not only have the police interviewed him most searchingly, but they have indicated that he must be prepared to be seen again. They cannot have found anything against him, and I am sure it will remain so. But supposing the Cloudsdale disappearance is never solved? Suspicion will always hang over a number of men, and Emmett most of all. His entire career, any hope of future promotion, even his wedding plans, must be in doubt.'

'Does Mrs Cloudsdale know the secret nature of her husband's work?' asked Holmes.

'I believe not. She is just agitated that he has not returned home.'

'Would she be willing to speak to me?'

'She would be willing to speak to anyone who might be of some assistance. I can introduce you. I know of a rather nice little tea shop much frequented by respectable ladies. Quiet, select — excellent pastries. I shall book a table for three.'

'Four,' said Holmes.

CHAPTER TWO

'I think your brother has the same observational skill as you, Holmes,' I said, once Mycroft had departed.

'He does, and to a higher degree than I,' said Holmes. This comment was rather startling as I had never before heard Holmes admit to anyone having a better mind than he. In fact, I am sure I have never heard it since.

'Does he go about solving mysteries?' I asked.

'He does not. For him, deductions are too simple, they are almost a trick he does for his own amusement. You may have observed that when I encounter a particularly knotty problem, I like to sit quietly with a pipe or two and reflect on what I know or can deduce; the incontrovertible facts, the impossibilities which can be safely discarded, the conclusions which must remain. To Mycroft such exercises are unnecessary, the conclusions are so obvious to him that he does not need to exert himself.'

'Have you ever collaborated with your brother on a mystery?' I asked.

'Not as such,' said Holmes. 'I have occasionally when so engaged, paid him a visit, laid the facts before him, and asked for his opinion. Sometimes he will provide a complete answer from his armchair, and then it is up to me to find the proof. He is invariably correct. But he has no interest in pursuing criminals for the satisfaction of apprehending them. What has involved him in this particular case is the fate of his old friend.'

It was then that I thought if anyone could solve this mystery it was not simply Holmes but the combination of two of the greatest minds the world has ever known. I am not a great mind, as my readers will be well aware, but the prospect of seeing Holmes and Mycroft working together was undeniably thrilling.

The tea shop was as described by Mycroft Holmes, with small tables laid with white linen cloths, and lace curtains at the windows. We had no fear of being overheard as he had secured a table in a quiet alcove. It was a place for gentle conversation and secret whispers over china teacups with the soothing application of a hot beverage and cream-filled pastries. Mycroft placed an order for afternoon tea with a cake tray, and while we waited for them to be brought, I studied Mrs Cloudsdale. Everything about her was sombre — her expression, her clothing, and the careful arrangement of her hair under a small dark bonnet. Her manner was the epitome of a concerned wife. She was making a valiant effort to be as helpful as possible, knowing how important it was to be firm and practical, while reserving her deeper, more anguished emotions for the privacy of home.

She had brought a photograph of her husband, taken with their eldest son on the occasion of his departure for Cambridge. Holmes studied it intently. I sometimes wondered if he had a mind like a camera, able to commit detailed pictures to his memory so they were always available to be brought out for examination. There was nothing about the missing Mr Cloudsdale that was remarkable, either in his build, clothing or features, and I feared that any advertisement for sightings would provoke a torrent of responses which would only impede enquiries.

'I am sure,' Holmes began, 'that you have spoken about your husband many times in the last three weeks, described his appearance, his character, his interests and his tastes. But I would be grateful if you could tell me about him.'

'Of course,' she said. 'Anthony and I have been married twenty-two years. We have a small house in Pimlico, about a mile from his office. He started working in Whitehall at first as a junior clerk, but over the years he has been promoted several times and has always enjoyed the trust of his superiors. He is a kind, gentle, very steady man. I cannot imagine that he would do anything dishonourable. He liked tidiness and routine; some might say he abhorred upset and any disturbance of his usual habits. To disappear as he has done is so far from his character that I can only think some catastrophe has happened.'

'Was there anything at all unusual about his behaviour on the day you last saw him?'

'No, nothing at all. He rose at his usual hour, then washed and dressed as he always did, ate the same breakfast —'

'Which was?'

'Kippers, a poached egg, toast and preserves, tea. He left the house at the usual time.'

'Does he walk to the office?'

'Yes, in all weathers — he says the walk is good for the constitution. Since he sits at a desk all day, he likes to be active in his leisure time.'

'Was there anything unusual on his mind? A personal worry? His health? Concerns about his work?'

Mrs Cloudsdale gave this some thought. 'I have wondered a great deal about that. We had discussed the expenses associated with our daughter's wardrobe, and our eldest boy's education, but there was nothing we needed to be concerned about. We have always been prudent with such things, accumulated funds for those requirements we could anticipate and reserved additional savings for the unexpected. We have always been quite comfortable. His health was good — had there been anything troubling his mind regarding that, I am sure he would have shared it with me. Our doctor has told me that Anthony had not consulted him recently. He attends a gymnasium twice a week. A reputable establishment for gentlemen in Pall Mall. As to his work, well, that was not something we discussed in any detail.'

'No pressing matters that day?'

'No, in fact —' she paused before continuing — 'rather the opposite, I think. Anthony likes to feel useful, trusted. That always puts him in an especially cheerful mood. He works directly for Sir Crawford Yates, who is a very important man. He had been particularly busy throughout the previous week, and while he could not say what he was engaged in, I know he was proud of his service. I would say that was how he was that morning.'

'I assume you have already shown this picture to the police and supplied them with a full description?'

'Yes, I have. I suppose they have alerted constables to look out for him. I can't help thinking he must have suffered an accident and lost his memory. He may be in a hospital somewhere.' She sighed. 'But you see from his portrait there is nothing to make him stand out from so many other men in the same profession. He is five feet seven inches in height and of a good build, neither too thin nor too portly. You can't see it on the photograph, but there is a wart on the left side of his nose. And he has a scar on his right knee — a childhood accident.'

'I know this may be hard for you,' said Holmes, carefully, 'but do try and think of anything, however trivial, that was in the slightest way unusual — perhaps in the last two months. Did your husband make a purchase? Was there something he read in the newspaper and commented upon? Or a situation, either good or troubling, regarding a member of his family or a friend or colleague.'

Mrs Cloudsdale fell into a thoughtful silence. We refreshed the pot of tea and Mycroft finished the last of the cake.

It was Mycroft who saw that Mrs Cloudsdale was staring at the pattern painted on the china teacups, clusters of pink roses. 'What delightful flowers,' he said.

'Yes,' she agreed, 'but they are pink.'

'What colour would you prefer?' he asked.

'It isn't that; I was reminded of something. But it was all a mistake, and I had quite put it out of my mind.'

'Even if a circumstance has no bearing at all on the matter in hand, it is best to consider it, so it may be laid aside and not hamper our efforts,' said Holmes.

'It was a conversation with my cousin Hilda, about a month ago,' she said. 'Hilda came to have tea one afternoon, and she said that she had seen Anthony going into a tea shop with our daughter Lettie a few days earlier. Neither of them had mentioned this to me, and I asked Hilda when that was, and it so happened that on that date, Lettie and I were out shopping the whole day. I felt sure Hilda was mistaken. She claimed that Lettie was wearing a hat decorated with yellow flowers, and my daughter does not own such a hat.'

'Where was this tea shop?' asked Mycroft.

'I think it was near St James's Park, not far from Whitehall.'

Mycroft nodded knowingly but said nothing.

'As far as I am aware, neither Anthony nor Lettie have ever been there,' Mrs Cloudsdale continued. 'I was about to tell Hilda she must be mistaken, but then I decided it would be better not to. She had formed the impression that Anthony was with our daughter, and if I had questioned her, and said it could not have been Lettie, she might have placed a different construction on what she saw. I think she must have seen another man entirely. I should explain that Hilda is short-sighted and rather vain about wearing spectacles. I did not want to call attention to her eyesight, about which she is extremely sensitive. So, I said nothing and simply allowed Hilda to think she had seen Anthony and Lettie.'

'Did you make any mention of it to either your husband or your daughter?' asked Holmes.

'I did mention the tea shop as one I had heard recommended. Neither of them said anything about it. I decided that Hilda must have made a mistake and put it out of my mind.'

'Did you mention it to the police?' asked Holmes.

'No, I didn't.'

'I agree that the most likely explanation is that your cousin was mistaken, and the matter is of no importance whatsoever,' said Holmes. 'However, I would urge you to advise the police. If you do not, and they were to learn of it, they might conclude that you thought there was something in it and had deliberately concealed it.'

Mrs Cloudsdale reluctantly agreed.

Once she had departed, Holmes and Mycroft entered into a debate. The unpleasant possibility that cousin Hilda had been correct, and Mr Cloudsdale's disappearance had a scandalous explanation, was aired. The brothers decided to pool their resources in the case, and it was agreed that they would meet at regular intervals in a private room at Mycroft's club, which was near his lodgings in Pall Mall, to share their findings. I sensed that Mycroft was puzzled at my inclusion in their deliberations. He was not sure what I could add to the endeavour, but Holmes's reassurance that I was trustworthy and had assisted him in previous cases, overcame his initial concerns. I think

Mycroft saw me as an example of the thinking of the common man. How valuable he considered such a viewpoint I am not sure, but I believe it did help Holmes's enquiries to add a measure of down-to-earth sense to his elevated and often impenetrable ruminations.

CHAPTER THREE

'The inevitable pall of secrecy which occludes so much of this case is a severe impediment,' said Holmes. We were at his Montague Street rooms, and he was perusing that part of his collection of newspapers which covered the period in which Cloudsdale had disappeared, hoping to find something of significance. 'We do not know where he was going, only that he arrived there, and it was not too far distant as he was expected back the same day. We do not know how he travelled. We do not know the nature of what he was carrying, which would offer us a clue. Is it possible that the papers were not copied at all, but a similar set substituted? No-one can or will tell us.' His irritation at not being made privy to sensitive government secrets was transparent.

I was permitted to help him examine the newspapers as he handed them to me one by one, but remained under strict instructions not to interfere with the order in which they had been arranged, and simply return them to Holmes with my observations when I was done. 'What am I looking for?' I asked.

'You know my collection, and my interests,' he said. 'Describe anything out of the common way, even the smallest piece that catches the eye, and might offer some suggestion as to the fate of Mr Cloudsdale.'

I did think of saying that it was the uncommon rather than the ordinary which was believed to attract readers of newspapers, or the publishers might not have sold many copies. The sensational, and the outré, resulted in the kind of articles Holmes cut out for his collection, with the everyday commerce delegated to advertisements, while the grumbles and irritations of daily existence resided in readers' correspondence.

So far, we had found nothing to suggest that an unidentified body of a man had been found, or an accident or crime had occurred in which an unconscious victim had been removed to hospital. Neither were there any urgent appeals for sightings of young ladies who had abruptly left home in the company of an older man.

One topic which I thought to mention, since it had given rise to an energetic debate, was the behaviour of cab drivers. This battalion of hard-working men who plied their trade in all weathers for the convenience of gentlefolk, was all too easy to blame for one's own carelessness in the face of heavy traffic. A recent accident to a child who had run into a busy road and been fortunate to escape with minor contusions, had lit the fuse of indignation in the correspondence columns of the London press, with examples being provided of similar events which the public was instructed to deplore.

'I cannot find any account of a gentleman being hurt in a carriage accident,' I said, 'although there was an argument about one who only narrowly avoided injury.'

I was continuing my perusal of this paper, but Holmes, with that little flicker of interest in his eyes I had come to recognise, took it from me, and read the item intently. 'The correspondent says that the man, of respectable appearance, had not alighted from the cab, but was making his way on foot towards Stepney railway station, when he slipped, and was very nearly crushed under the wheels,' said Holmes. 'He went to assist the man who was shaken but unhurt and refused all help. A crowd gathered to remonstrate with the driver, who denied that he was at fault, claiming that the man had stumbled into his path.'

'There is no description of the man,' I said.

'No, but let us see if later editions carry any further details.'

What followed was two columns of letters which were mainly general complaints, but we were able to learn a little more about the incident. The man had not given any personal details and when the furore was over, he had vanished. It was thought he must have been hurrying to catch a train. A policeman who was on point near the station had been attracted by the noise of the crowd and came to discover the reason for all the excitement. Another witness to the event said that it was not the cabdriver's fault, but the man had simply stumbled as the ground was slippery with recent rain. Still another witness said it was not the man who had almost been hit who had stumbled, but another man, who had bumped into him, knocking him into the path of the cab. Satisfied that no crime had been committed, and no-one was hurt, the policeman had simply calmed the crowd and advised them to disperse. Neither the hurrying man nor the one who had slipped and knocked him over were still there to be questioned.

'Could one of these two men have been Cloudsdale?' I asked. 'If the event was assumed to be an accident and no harm done, it would not have been reported by the police except locally.'

Holmes delved into a gazetteer of London. 'Stepney station,' he said, 'near Limehouse docks. Factories and warehouses. Mycroft might be able to tell us more. Unfortunately, the letter writers are vague about the date and time, but it is not impossible that one of the men in question is Cloudsdale. I will write to Sergeant Lestrade advising him to speak to the constable who dealt with that incident.'

When Holmes and Mycroft next met there was much poring over maps, directories, and train timetables. 'The destination does not surprise me,' said Mycroft. 'The area is almost wholly devoted to industry. Flour mills, chemical refineries, production of undersea cables, iron works, and warehousing, to name just a few. There are new ones being established all the time. It is a prime area for receiving and storing imported materials. I would not be at all surprised if one or more of these companies had a contract with the government to develop and produce products which other countries would like to know about and pay well for the secret.'

'Until we learn otherwise, we must start with the assumption that Cloudsdale's destination was one of the factories near the station,' said Holmes. 'If the papers were either copied, which would have been a laborious procedure, or more likely substituted for others, how would we know if that had occurred?'

'I have broached that subject,' said Mycroft, with a smile, 'and the only response I received was that we would know.'

'I hope Emmett is bearing up under the anxiety,' I said.

'Poor fellow, it is weighing heavily upon him. He prays every day for Cloudsdale to be found safe. I think it might help him if he was to speak with you, Sherlock. Once you meet him you will be as certain as I am that he has nothing to do with this affair.'

Holmes was confident that once Sergeant Lestrade knew he was interested in the case a visit would follow, and he was correct. The sergeant was careful not to let it be generally known that he consulted an amateur detective, especially as Holmes was generous enough to allow him full credit for the results of their joint efforts. Holmes received a note to arrange a private meeting, which took place at my rooms in Farringdon. Mycroft, due to his government post, had decided not to reveal his involvement in the enquiry and did not attend.

'I had an interesting interview with Mrs Cloudsdale just recently,' said Lestrade, as we sat around the table with tea and a plate of buns. 'She told me a strange tale of a young lady with yellow flowers in her hat who was not her daughter, but then she assured me that it had no importance at all with regard to her husband, and you told her so.' He chuckled. 'What am I to make of that?'

'I am afraid that the truth of that may never be known until we are able to interview Mr Cloudsdale,' said Holmes, diplomatically.

'You may well be right,' said Lestrade, 'a situation I look forward to.' He took a gulp of tea. 'Will your brother not be joining us? I had the pleasure of interviewing him recently. I assume he has told you all he knows or is permitted to say about Mr Cloudsdale's mission?'

'He has,' said Holmes. 'In view of the nature of his occupation he prefers to take a more observational role. He is constantly on the alert for news, and should he happen to learn anything of interest to the enquiry he will of course communicate it at once.'

'Very sensible,' said Lestrade. 'I am indebted to you for your note about the incident outside Stepney railway station,' he went on. 'I should emphasise that as far as the police are concerned, the Cloudsdale business is simply a search for a missing man. We do not, at least at my level, concern ourselves with issues of national security. In any case, it does not appear that the papers Mr Cloudsdale was carrying were stolen, a source of great relief to all concerned, so I have been told.'

'I have considered the possibility that at some point, the envelope being carried by Mr Cloudsdale was opened, the papers stolen, and others substituted,' said Holmes. 'It might have occurred at any stage in his journey, or even before he left the office.'

Lestrade nodded. 'I have been told that Mr Cloudsdale arrived at his appointed destination a mere half an hour after the agreed time. A great deal of work has been going on to which I am not privy, but the result is that the most senior government advisors are quite certain after examining all the material in question, that the papers delivered by Mr Cloudsdale were the original ones. Nothing has been altered, or added, or substituted. During their creation they were kept very secure. They were held in a safe until the moment they were handed to Cloudsdale for delivery. I am also told that the volume of the material makes it impossible for a copy to have been made during the course of Cloudsdale's journey. Cloudsdale might have opened the seal to look at the papers himself, though why he would have done so, we cannot tell. He might have shown them to another person, who was not authorised to see them, which would be very upsetting and, so I have been told, quite out of character. The only thing I have learned is that he made his way to the delivery place by train.'

'Have there been any sightings of him since he disappeared?' I asked.

'Any number,' said Lestrade, with a weary sigh. 'We are looking into them all. But he was not a distinctive figure. He was of average height and build, dressed like many other gentlemen of his class, and adopted the most common fashion of whiskers. I would only be prepared to trust a report if the witness knew him personally or saw him up close. He had a wart on his nose,' he added gloomily.

'He attended a gymnasium twice a week,' said Holmes.

'Yes, and it is a respectable club for gentlemen. He was last seen there the week before he disappeared, and none of the officers or members have seen him or know where he might be. I believe they are being truthful.'

'Do you have a description of the man seen at Stepney?' asked Holmes.

'The constable present at that incident made a note of it, but it was more of a public order issue as the crowd was busy deciding who to blame, and things were getting rather heated,' said Lestrade. 'The one thing I can tell you is that the time it took place did fit the time shortly after Mr Cloudsdale delivered his envelope, and the man was described as medium height, respectably dressed and in his forties. If it was Cloudsdale, he would have boarded the train at Stepney taking the route back to Charing Cross, which is just a few minutes' walk from Whitehall. The constable came on the scene after the man had hurried into the station, so didn't see him. He was reassured by the crowd that the man was unhurt. He would have liked to speak to him, but by then the train was already on its way.'

'And he was sure it was an accident?' asked Holmes.

'It was hard to be sure of anything,' said Lestrade. 'It all happened very quickly. The cab driver said the hurrying man had dashed in front of him and he was lucky not to be struck. But there was another man involved, a much younger man. Some of the crowd said this man had slipped and fallen against the hurrying man, so projecting him into danger. One person actually said he thought the younger man had deliberately pushed the older man into the path of the cab.'

'The newspapers state that the young man was not available for interview,' said Holmes.

'No, he had left the scene by the time the constable arrived. He seemed very eager to get away, although he might just have wanted to catch the train.'

'Did he follow the older man onto the train?'

'We don't know.'

'Is there a description?'

'Short, but strongly made, very fast on his feet, clean shaven. Age about twenty. But if Cloudsdale had left on the train at Stepney, where did he go afterwards? A man hurrying for a train is not an unusual sight. The Stepney police are making enquiries in case anyone saw him or the younger fellow. That is all I can tell you.'

'And there have been no incidents reported on the trains leaving Stepney? No quarrels or struggles?'

'We have learned of none so far.'

'If Cloudsdale was being pursued, he might have alighted at a station earlier than planned,' I said. 'Perhaps he never went as far as Charing Cross.'

'Otherwise, if he did reach Charing Cross, why did he not return to the office or report the incident?' said Holmes. 'Was he a frightened man who thought that someone had just attempted to murder him?'

'But Sergeant, are the police now satisfied that no-one at Whitehall could have been involved in this disappearance?' I asked.

'Far from it,' said Lestrade. 'Most men were at work on the day Cloudsdale disappeared. There were some absent though illness, or attending public events, all of which we have been able to confirm. We are now looking at those who have said they were travelling as they will need to establish where they were. But even if everyone can be accounted for at the time of Mr Cloudsdale's disappearance, that does not mean there are no criminals under our very noses. The business of gentlemen at their desks is not brute violence but information. And they can be as guilty as anyone else.'

CHAPTER FOUR

Our next meeting with Mycroft Holmes was in the same tea shop where we had interviewed Mrs Cloudsdale. He had arranged for us to take tea with Joshua Emmett, but we had gathered around the table some minutes before his friend's appointed arrival to share information. Mycroft told us that he had paid a visit to the tea shop near St James's Park where Mrs Cloudsdale's cousin Hilda claimed to have seen Mr Cloudsdale in company with a lady wearing a hat with yellow flowers. 'Neither of those individuals appeared, I am sorry to say, and I did not wish to attract attention to myself by asking questions,' he said. 'It was a small establishment, rather dark, with indifferent pastries, and much favoured by persons, usually a gentleman accompanied by a lady, who did not appear to me to wish to be seen. As a single gentleman any enquiry I might have made about a lady, would have been misinterpreted.'

We shared with him all that we had learned from Sergeant Lestrade concerning the incident at Stepney station, with the hope that police questioning would elicit some details as to what if anything took place on the train. 'It is more than ever of moment that you speak to Emmett,' added Mycroft. 'He has been questioned further and has encountered a difficulty which I hope we can resolve for him.'

As he spoke, Mr Joshua Emmett appeared. He was aged about thirty, with good features and soulful brown eyes. There was nothing remarkable about his appearance and I think that even the dullest wit on seeing him, judging by his neatness of grooming and style of attire, would have at once guessed correctly that he was a clerk. I have an interest in gentlemen's fine tailoring; in my student days I studied clothing of quality through the windows of emporiums I did not yet have the funds to enter. Emmett's suit was probably the best he could afford, but it was far from new, and very carefully maintained to keep it fresh as long as possible. The notable thing about him was that he was not alone. The lady who he conducted to our table was little more than twenty, modestly clad, with pretty blue eyes and an expression of disarming sweetness. Her gown, of a leaf green hue, was nicely set off by a bonnet of darker green, decorated with a spray of yellow silk roses.

'Gentlemen, I am most grateful that you have agreed to see me,' said Emmett. 'Allow me to introduce my fiancée, Miss Millicent Jessup,' he added proudly, as we rose to greet her.

The usual bland politenesses tumbled from our lips, and we were all seated, but to a man none of us could tear our gaze from the spray of yellow roses.

Mycroft ordered tea, and as we waited something impelled me to break the awkward silence.

'What a very charming bonnet, Miss Jessup,' I exclaimed.

'Why, thank you,' she said. I dared not look at Holmes or his brother as I could almost feel their hard stares of disapproval burning into me.

'My cousin Lily simply adores bonnets,' I went on, blithely, 'she says she can never have too many, and if she was here, now, I know she would be demanding to know where you purchased the one you are wearing as she would want to have one just like it.'

Miss Jessup uttered a cheerful little laugh. 'Oh, how kind of you to say so! But it cannot be purchased anywhere, as I trimmed it myself.'

'Then it is the only one of its kind?'

'There is one other that I know of. It was worn by a lady I saw in the street.' She turned to Emmett. 'You must remember her, dear? The lady who dropped the parcels?'

'Oh — I am not sure,' said Emmett, vaguely. 'My memory for bonnets is not very extensive.'

She patted his arm affectionately. 'Dear Joshua, he is so very kind. A lady spilled all her parcels in the street right in front of him, and he was good enough to help pick them up and restore them to her. I had time to study her bonnet and since I make silk flowers, I thought I could trim up my plain one. The result,' and she framed her bonnet with her hands like a picture, 'you see.'

'How perfectly lovely!' I said. 'Was the lady known to you?'

'No, not at all.'

'Do tell me if you chance to see her again so I can discover where she purchased her bonnet, and I will buy one for my cousin for her birthday,' I said.

This little matter having been disposed of, Holmes and Mycroft breathed more easily, and the tea and dainties that appeared on the table occupied our attention until Mr Emmett began to speak of what concerned him.

'Mr Holmes,' he began, 'your brother, with the concern of an old and valued friend, has suggested I meet you to discuss something which troubles me and to which you might offer a solution.'

'I am happy to oblige,' said Holmes. 'Does this have anything to do with the disappearance of Mr Cloudsdale, or another matter entirely?'

'I am quite sure it can have no connection to that unfortunate circumstance,' said Emmett. 'I am told that the police are no further forward in finding him and we are all anxiously waiting to hear something, hoping most fervently that it will be good news.'

'Then kindly tell me what your question is,' said Holmes.

'As you must know,' Emmett began, 'we at the Whitehall offices have all been asked by the police if we had any information relating to Mr Cloudsdale. One of the questions put to each of us concerned our personal circumstances, our income, investments, and expenses. Of course, I have nothing to hide. I am a bachelor; I live with my mother, who is a widow. Miss Jessup and I have known each other for five years and have only recently announced our betrothal. Marriage can be an expensive venture and I was asked about my salary, and if that was my only income. I was also asked about the Jessup family and their circumstances.' He glanced at his fiancée.

Miss Jessup smiled understandingly. 'My father was once in the business of construction,' she said, 'but a bad fall put an end to that, and we have to make do as best we can.'

'I told them everything,' said Emmett. 'My salary and the interest on some small savings are all my regular income. The thing is — and I suppose I was being excessively honest, I was obliged to mention a sum of money I received recently, which was quite unexpected.'

He took a deep breath.

'It was about three weeks ago. An envelope was delivered to our home. There was no stamp so it must have come by hand. On the front of the envelope was written my name, and the words, 'with thanks.' When I opened it, I found inside to my great surprise a fifty-pound banknote. That was all. There was no letter, nothing to indicate who had sent it or why. Of course, it was very welcome and appeared to have been meant for me, but I could not imagine who my benefactor might be. I showed the envelope to my mother and to Millie, but neither could suggest anything.' He turned to Miss Jessup. 'You recall, my dear, how astonished I was to receive the money.'

'I do indeed,' said Miss Jessup. 'In fact, you even wondered if there had been a mistake, and it was meant for another man of the same or similar name. But you said you would not spend it and keep it safe in case it was ever claimed.'

'I did,' said Emmett. 'I paid the money into my bank. When I told the police about this they asked if I had any idea who might have sent it and on further thought I recalled that some years ago, a cousin of mine, Charles Guthrie, who had been very hard pressed, had asked me for a loan. It so happened that I had reached the age of majority and come into a small inheritance from my late grandfather. I therefore loaned Guthrie the sum he required. Thirty pounds. He was very grateful and said that he intended to start up in trade, work hard and accumulate funds, and, once he was able, he would repay the loan with interest. That seemed to be the best explanation. The police asked me to confirm what I had told them, but I could not. I asked my mother if she knew where cousin Charles lived or worked, but she said she had not heard from him for several years. I went to his last known residence, but the family had gone away quite some time ago, leaving no forwarding address. Yesterday a policeman came and asked me if I had found the proof they had asked of me, but I had not. I showed him the envelope, but that proved nothing. I had to ask for more time, but I feel that they regard the whole matter with suspicion. That is the second time they have interviewed me, and it is not a pleasant experience.'

'May I see the envelope?' asked Holmes.

Emmett produced it, and Holmes laid it on the table before us, and carefully studied it on both front and back and also inside with his magnifying glass. Emmett's name and the words 'with thanks' were written in pencil in capital letters.

'Plain weave envelope of a cheap common type, a halfpenny at any stationer's,' he said. 'A few light marks usual in such missives when handled by delivery boys. The use of the pencil and capitals rather than cursive in ink is very suggestive. The writer wished to conceal the identity of the sender. If it was the repayment of a loan, one might ask why that was thought to be necessary. Surely the debtor would want you to know he had cleared the debt. I would also have expected him to have inserted a message to that effect. Have you ever received anything of this nature before?'

'No, never.'

'If you receive another such envelope, you must take it to the police unopened.'

'I will.'

'On what day did you receive it?'

'I am not sure I can remember.'

'Was it the same day you mentioned it to me?' asked Miss Jessup.

'I think — it was the day before.'

Miss Jessup produced a pocket diary from her reticule and consulted it. 'Yes, it was so unusual I made a note. Here it is. "Joshua has received a great surprise of fifty pounds. Still no news of Mr Cloudsdale."' She showed the page to Holmes, who noted the date. The envelope had been delivered on the Wednesday morning, two days after Cloudsdale's disappearance.

'What would you like me to do?' Holmes asked Emmett.

'I suppose — if you could find Charles Guthrie and ask him to confirm that he sent it? Otherwise, I have no explanation.'

Holmes leaned back in his chair, pressing his fingertips together, in thoughtful pose. 'Tell me about Guthrie.'

'He is my first cousin, and he would now be aged about forty. He has never settled to any occupation, and I fear he may have erred into areas which, while not actually criminal, would have made him some bad companions. The last I heard of him, which was some years ago, he was peddling cheap jewellery. He always said if he could only have a good start in business, he would make his fortune.'

'Did your mother ever loan him money?'

'She would never admit it, but I rather think she did. She was fond of him, and I suppose wanted to keep him on the path of honesty.'

'Can you suggest how he might have accumulated fifty pounds?'

'I really don't know. A lucky wager perhaps?'

From the expressions around me, I could see that none at the table regarded that as at all promising.

'This fifty-pound note — was it clean or dirty? Smooth or crumpled?' asked Holmes.

'It was clean,' said Emmett. 'In fact, it looked quite new.'

'Not from a bundle carried by a betting man, then,' said Holmes. 'Again, some effort has been made to prevent you or anyone else from tracing the origins of this payment. All we know for certain at present is that you paid the sum into your bank.'

Emmett looked unhappy. 'Let us see what we can discover,' said Mycroft, soothingly.

With promises from both the Holmes brothers, the meeting ended with tea and cake. Emmett provided us with his card, and Miss Jessup smiled encouragement. My only thought was that while Emmett was unlikely to be endangered by what we had learned, he could never be entirely safe from suspicion until Cloudsdale was found and was able to explain himself.

'If it was Guthrie and he had come by the money through unlawful means, he might want to conceal its origins,' said Holmes once the betrothed couple had left us. His tone of voice made it apparent that he was not confident of this as an explanation. 'But who delivered it? Not a street urchin, making pennies from such work, or the envelope would be much more soiled than it is. The sender himself? I doubt it. Why take such elaborate precautions and then risk being seen? Is there a telegraph office nearby? If so, a reliable boy might have been hired from there. Stamford, I have a task for you. Make enquiries at the local telegraph offices to see if there was a boy hired to deliver a private message to Mr Emmett.'

I suppose haunting telegraph offices near Emmett's lodgings was a humble enough mission considered suitable for me. I was not entirely happy about that. While these delivery boys were for the most part diligent and well behaved, looking smartly official in their uniforms, there were some who supplemented their wages by other means, not all of which were strictly honest. In making enquiries for a boy who made additional deliveries, I would have to choose my words very carefully.

CHAPTER FIVE

It was not until the following day that Holmes and I were able once more to meet with Sergeant Lestrade, who had been actively involved in the search for Cloudsdale. He came to my lodgings looking exhausted and in need of refreshment, which I was happy to provide. Holmes was often dismissive about the efforts of the police, and Lestrade's abilities in particular, but I thought that the two men had more in common than Holmes would have liked to admit. They both had a dogged determination to see an enquiry through to the end, and an extraordinary capacity for hard work.

I was obliged to report that my efforts to find the delivery boy had so far proved unsuccessful, but I had left my card at the telegraph offices in case he might be tempted to appear. 'Mr Emmett has been wondering if his mysterious benefactor might have been a cousin, Charles Guthrie,' said Holmes. 'If Guthrie had acquired the money by dubious means, he might well have wished to conceal both its source and his whereabouts from his family. I would like to trace him. Do you have any information which might assist me?'

'That I do,' said Lestrade. 'Emmett's family had good reason to be ashamed of him. His last known occupation was running an illegal betting business. He didn't make his fortune and was sent to prison three years ago. He served eighteen months before he died of a lung complaint.'

'Ah,' said Holmes. 'It appears that Mr Emmett was unaware of this.'

'Really?' said Lestrade, dubiously. 'Well, his mother was the next of kin, and she had to scrape together the means for a funeral. But the result is we can now show that the money cannot have come from the cousin. In fact, we only have Mr Emmett's word for it that it was delivered to his door. He might have written that envelope himself. Maybe he knows full well where the money came from and isn't prepared to say.'

Holmes frowned at this last observation but said nothing.

'And then,' Lestrade went on, 'we have this mysterious lady with the yellow flowers in her hat. Who is she? I have learned very recently that Miss Jessup has a hat of the same description, and her explanation is that she copied it from a lady in the street who dropped her parcels on the ground. Could this lady be a spy and it was a method of passing secret messages? Or perhaps she does not exist at all, and Mr Emmett and Miss Jessup are not telling the truth, and Miss Jessup is in fact the lady who was seen with Mr Cloudsdale?'

'That is pure speculation,' said Holmes, cautiously, but he appeared unsettled, as if the thought had been in his mind too and he had not wanted it aired.

'Have you discovered anything further regarding Mr Cloudsdale?' I asked.

'A few indications, no more,' said Lestrade. 'We now have a better description of the hurrying man at Stepney station which strengthens our suspicion that he might have been Cloudsdale. And I have spoken to a lady who was on the train when it stopped at Stepney. She saw a very agitated man jump aboard with moments to spare before the train drew away.'

'Did she see anyone following him?' asked Holmes.

'It is hard to tell if a man is chasing another man or the train. But she did notice a young man run onto the platform and just miss the train as it pulled away, and he looked very annoyed.'

'Where did the first man alight? Does she remember?'

'It so happened that she watched him, fearing he might be unwell, but he simply rested to get his breath back, then he alighted at Fenchurch Street. If that was Cloudsdale, it is where he would have got the Charing Cross train. That is the last possible sighting we have.'

'Then we cannot be sure if he actually caught the train to Charing Cross or another train, or left the station at Fenchurch Street,' Holmes observed.

'Not at present, no.'

At that moment there was a knock at my door and my landlady peered in. 'Mr Stamford, there is a telegraph boy says he has a message for you. But it is not a telegram. Shall I show him up?'

'Please do,' I said. 'And bring another teacup.'

The boy who appeared was about eleven or twelve years of age, in uniform and with a canvas bag around his shoulders like a post sack. He looked rather taken aback to find three men present, and I was relieved that Lestrade was in plain clothes, or the boy might have taken fright and run away.

'Mr Stamford?' he asked anxiously. 'The gentleman who wants to know who took a letter to Mr Emmett?'

'Yes, do come in, I understand you have something to tell me,' I said.

The boy crept in and sat down. I saw him eyeing the tea things and as soon as the extra cup arrived, I poured tea for him which he gulped eagerly, adding rather more sugar than was usual. He needed no prompting to take a bread bun, stuff it with a slice of ham, and wash down the hearty bites with his tea. In between bites he was persuaded to provide his name, which was Joe.

'I don't usually take other letters,' he said, wiping his mouth, 'but the lady was very nice and promised me a shilling.'

'A lady, was it?' asked Lestrade.

'Yes, sir.'

'Can you describe her?'

'Well, she was very friendly. But she wore a veil, so I didn't see a lot of her face. I thought from her voice that she was a young lady.'

'How was she dressed?'

'Like a lady. That's all I can remember.'

'And she gave you the envelope?'

'Yes.'

'What was written on it?'

'The man's name, and some other words.'

'Ink or pencil?'

'Pencil. Big letters. She gave me sixpence straight away and said if I went and came back double quick, I would get another one. And I did.'

'How did she speak?' asked Holmes. 'Was she English or a foreigner?'

'English — I'd say she was a Londoner,' said Joe. 'Oh, and she gave me something else.' He dug his hand in his pocket, and to our astonishment pulled out a flower made of paper. It was a yellow rosebud. 'She said I could put it in my buttonhole, and look like a gent.'

'How remarkable!' I exclaimed.

'Young man,' said Holmes, 'you have done very well to come here. Here is sixpence for you, and if you ever see that lady again, try to remember how she is dressed, her gown, her hat, and so on, and if you find out anything about her, I will give you a shilling.'

The next time we saw Mycroft he had some new developments to report, and it seemed that it was not only the police who were casting suspicious eyes on his friend.

CHAPTER SIX

An urgent note summoned both Holmes and me to Mycroft's club that evening. It was situated not far from Whitehall, with a small portico, a deferential doorman and a relentlessly masculine interior. There was a sombre dining room, an even more sombre lounge where waiters would bring brandy, cigars and newspapers to the members' armchairs, and small meeting rooms, one of which we occupied. A dignified servant brought us drinks, a plate of savoury tartlets, and three copies of that morning's *Times*, and left us to our business.

'There has been some excitement in Whitehall today,' said Mycroft. 'I have not of course been told the reason for it, but I keep myself alert for fragments which I can assemble into a convincing picture.'

'Has Cloudsdale been found?' I asked, eagerly.

'Regrettably, no, there is no news on that front, although the police do provide us with regular briefings. There is a Chief Inspector leading the case, by the name of Foinette. Today there was no visit from the police, but a very hurried meeting was called, and only the most senior men were in attendance. I saw them on their way, holding copies of this morning's *Times*.' He unrolled a copy on the table and passed the others to us. 'What, I wondered, could have excited them so? And why was it that when they left the meeting, they did not appear to be unhappy at what they had learned?'

'Do you have a conclusion?' asked Holmes.

'I do, but let me see if you come to the same one as I did.' He leaned back in his chair with a smile.

I could see that there was a well-established friendly rivalry between the brothers, to which I was unlikely to contribute. Nevertheless, I was ready to show willing, and started by studying the police court news.

There was a period of silence, disturbed only by the rustling of paper, until Holmes declared, 'Ah, I see it!' He pointed to a short paragraph. The subject was a Reuters telegram, stating that an explosion had taken place in the Baltic Sea.

'I concur,' said Mycroft. 'That is all we have thus far, but I hope the evening editions will be more informative. It is well known that naval exercises are carried out there, by steam-driven, ironclad vessels. Amongst other things, they conduct tests of new methods of propulsion, and weapons of war, such as mines and torpedoes. There are, as you might imagine, spies on shore with telescopes, studying the activities, gathering information and reporting on what they have seen. I suspect that what has occurred is a catastrophic failure of a recent test, and it does not involve a British vessel, which explains why Whitehall is not alarmed at the news. Might this be connected with the documents carried by Mr Cloudsdale? That meeting is very suggestive, and if there is a connection, it shows that at least part of the material he carried has been copied by some means we have yet to determine and put to use.'

Holmes and his brother lapsed into thought. I could almost hear the machinery of their brains turning, and wondered what extraordinary energy powered them. 'We have not learned the subject of Mr Cloudsdale's documents, or where he was taking them, but I think this event might throw some light on it,' said Holmes, at last. 'We know from the way the material was guarded and handled that it was highly sensitive. My first thought was that the papers included a description of a new weapon. It is more likely, however, given the short period of time before the material was employed, that it described an improvement of an existing one.'

'I agree,' said Mycroft. 'An endeavour of this nature would have been discussed and costed at Whitehall before ministerial approval could be given to commence production. The information with its seal of approval would then be transmitted to the manufacturer, which was Cloudsdale's task. Did an agent of an unfriendly country somehow obtain a view of the papers, and in the brief time available, was unable to make an accurate or complete copy, which has led to this disaster? That is to be established. I imagine the government will be very pleased and relieved that valuable secrets have not fallen in their entirety into hands for which it was not intended.'

'But we are left with two very serious difficulties,' said Holmes. 'First of all, we must find Cloudsdale. There is much we can learn from him. And a scheme of this kind cannot be carried out by a single individual. It is too complex, and dare I say it, too efficient. There will be a gang of criminals. They must be found and brought to justice. For the security of the country, and of course to exonerate the innocents who currently lie under suspicion.'

As we deliberated, a later edition of *The Times* was brought to us, which was more informative about the explosion. It was thought by observers that an ironclad warship must have been conducting test firings of a new type of experimental steerable torpedo in the Baltic. There had been an onboard explosion, causing the ship to sink, with considerable loss of life.

'There are heavy industries which carry out government contracts of all kinds, not all of them military, some of which are located in the very area to which we believe Cloudsdale travelled,' said Mycroft. 'I recall hearing a conversation a while ago, regarding work that was being done to develop and perfect a steerable torpedo. The Royal Arsenal at Woolwich must be principally involved in the construction of torpedoes, but other factories might have carried out supplementary work; the manufacture of materials or parts such as wires and cables.'

'The next question,' said Holmes, 'is where the papers were opened and viewed? Could the opening and resealing of the envelope have been carried out with such delicacy on a moving train? I should not like to attempt it. Neither is it the best place to copy a document. It must have occurred during some break in the journey. But would Cloudsdale have calmly sat by and allowed this?'

'From what we know of the man, that is most unlikely,' said Mycroft. 'Was he attacked, robbed and restrained?' He shook his head. 'No. If he had been waylaid on the route in such a fashion, but was then permitted to continue his mission to deliver the papers, which was essential in order to avoid suspicion that anything unusual had taken place, why did he not report it at his destination when he handed them over?'

'We cannot rule out the possibility that he was compliant in the process,' said Holmes.

'Some underhand means might have been used to ensure his compliance, such as a bribe, or a drug, or a threat against his family,' said Mycroft. 'But once that was done, it does seem, if he was indeed the individual who was almost killed outside Stepney station that the villains had no further use for him. He may be so thoroughly frightened that he is hiding. The police already suspect that. Mrs Cloudsdale has told me they searched every inch of their home in Pimlico in case he is there, and have demanded to know if he has another residence available, which he has not. And she thinks she is being watched, in case she receives messages and conducts secret meetings with him.'

'Did he have any valuables upon his person apart from the

papers?' asked Holmes.

'Mrs Cloudsdale has informed me that he wore a set of gold cufflinks, and carried a silver watch,' said Mycroft. 'She has described them to the police who will be making enquiries at the pawnshops.'

'Let us consider the journey we believe was undertaken by Cloudsdale on the day he disappeared,' Holmes continued. 'If he departed from Charing Cross which is most likely, as it is the nearest station to Whitehall, on his way to Stepney, he would change trains at Fenchurch Street. The trains from both stations depart at frequent intervals. Given the half hour delay in his arrival, there are several places where the tampering with the envelope might have happened. I had wondered if it had been done before he set out, by someone at Whitehall he knew and trusted, but we have been told that the papers he delivered were the originals and had been most carefully guarded. Also, if a copy had been made at Whitehall, then there would have been no need to involve Cloudsdale at all. He would simply have been allowed to deliver them as usual. No, events suggest that the only way to obtain sight of them was during his journey. One possible location is his walk between Whitehall and Charing Cross, in which case he would have taken a later train than usual. Or he took his usual train, and the tampering took place during the change at Fenchurch Street, or at another station on his route where he would not usually alight. Or he arrived at his intended destination at his usual time, and the copying of the papers took place at Stepney. If we can discover which of these locations is the correct one, it might lead us to the gang.'

'And thereby prove that Emmett was in no way involved,' said Mycroft. He sighed. 'I shall keep my ears open for whispers which may confirm or confound our suspicions.'

'I will consult Lestrade again, to see if the police have learned of any unusual incidents along Cloudsdale's route,' said Holmes. He rubbed his hands together briskly. 'There is much work to be done!'

'And now I must tell you of another development, and this one I find worrying,' said Mycroft. 'Earlier today, one of the senior officers at the Treasury, Sir Crawford Yates, called me to his room for a private meeting. What could it be? A promotion? No. A change of role conferring no significant advancement? No. It was worse than that — he wanted an informal discussion. A prospect which should always strike terror in the heart of any sane man. He is well aware that Emmett and I are old friends from our schooldays, and he wanted to know my opinion of him. I told him what I have told you; Emmett is an honest man and entirely worthy of trust. Yates had a number of searching questions which I answered. But I fear from the tone of his questioning that the unfounded police suspicions of my friend have been circulating around Whitehall, and have reached the highest levels, and Yates has been considering them.

'It so chanced that Yates has known Cloudsdale for a number of years, and he assured me that he was quite certain the man was an honest and dutiful servant of the government. He said he would stake his life on it. As we were still apparently being informal, I asked him if he had seen Cloudsdale on the day he disappeared, as I was interested to have his view on the man's mood and conduct. Yates said he had not seen him at all that day, as he had been attending a business luncheon, a rather lengthy affair as these things so often are, with a reception and talks in the morning, and a four-course meal at which he had delivered a speech to a hundred men. He seemed to me to be very careful to mention this, and I later looked in the newspapers to see if it had been reported, and indeed it had; he was lunching with the British Mercantile Association at the City Hotel in London Street.

'Since Yates was so forthcoming, I made bold to ask him if he believed that the tragedy in the Baltic was connected in any way with the papers Cloudsdale was carrying. Yates merely replied that he had not yet seen a full report, so could not comment on the incident. I rather think I cannot expect him to comment at all, but his tone made his meaning clear enough. There was a connection, but he is not to mention it to someone in my humble position. He did say, however, that it was generally believed by those familiar with the material, that the papers Cloudsdale had been carrying could not possibly have been copied in the short time the journey allowed. Only a very small and select group of men have studied the papers. He himself has not done so. In his opinion it is unthinkable that any of the men so entrusted would have agreed to peddle secrets to a foreign power.'

When I considered these observations, it appeared to me that the impossibility of copying the papers in so short a time seemed to have been contradicted by the suspicion that the explosion in the Baltic had something to do with the contents, or at least part of them, having been somehow transmitted elsewhere. That led me to have my own thoughts on the conundrum. Which led me to plan my own investigation.

CHAPTER SEVEN

When assisting Holmes in his enquiries, I often like to share my ideas and deductions with him, despite the fact that they are usually met with looks of scorn and expressions of outright derision. I have never let that hold me back. Sometimes, a word from me has ignited a spark in Holmes's mind and taken him on a path I had never intended, but which ultimately led him to the solution of a mystery. On this occasion I was faced with two brilliant detectives and felt that if I was to propose one of my more speculative ideas to the brothers, I would be humiliated beyond belief. I needed facts, not theories, and unusually, I had one significant advantage over my more intelligent friends — my recent visit to Paris. In particular, the shopping expedition in the Grands Magasins, and what I had learned there.

Both Holmes and Mycroft had dismissed any suggestion that the papers carried by Mr Cloudsdale had been copied by photography, the available light on that day being insufficient to obtain a good image in the time available. Not knowing a great deal about the science of photography, I decided to consult those who did.

In the 1870s photography had severe limitations, which improved very considerably over the next decade. In 1877 it was not possible to capture a sharp image quickly without the assistance of a source of bright light, and the best possible source was the sun. For this reason, photographic studios were provided with glass walls and ceilings to admit as much sunlight as possible, which could be enhanced by large reflectors.

I began by making enquiries at a nearby studio, and received confirmation of what I had already suspected, that the light of candles and gas lamps was quite inadequate for successful photography. In recent years some experiments had been carried out with burning magnesium ribbon, which briefly produced an intense burst of light, but it had limited use. It was unsuitable for indoor work since it filled the room with clouds of ash.

I had had a thought, however, based on what I had recently seen in Paris. One of the great shopping emporiums on the Rue de Rivoli, the Marengo Hall, had been brightly lit by a new invention, an improved version of the electrical arc lamp, the work of a Russian engineer named Pavel Jablochkoff. It was rumoured that these lamps would be used as illuminations in the following year's Paris Exhibition. I had asked about them during my visit as I was wondering if they might be used to provide better lighting in hospitals for surgical procedures. I was informed, however, that the brightness of arc lamps and the noise and heat they emitted meant that they were unsuitable for small indoor spaces, and much to the relief of gas supply companies, they were too expensive for domestic use. The Jablochkoff candles, as they were called, would necessarily be confined to lighting streets or large halls. The inventor, I was told, had demonstrated them in London at the West India Docks earlier that year, when they had made a favourable impression. It had been suggested that they would be useful in places such as wharves and railway yards.

I was now wondering whether arc lamps might prove to be the answer for which photographers had been searching, removing their dependence on the light of the sun. Perhaps their expertise had enabled them to overcome the limitations of these lamps for indoor use. If I had had that inspiration, then surely, I thought, a professional photographer would have thought of it, too. I therefore visited a number of photographic studios to ask about this possibility. For all I knew, some businesses might already be using them. I found that some photographers knew nothing of the new electrical lamps, and those who had said that they had never, as far as they knew, been used in photography. The main obstacles, I was told, were that the suitability of the light they emitted for photography had yet to be proven and even if it was, adoption of the process would involve businesses in the expense not only of procuring the lamps themselves, but of installing steam engines or preferably, electrical dynamo machines to power them. Not every business had sufficient accommodation to house such devices. The strangest reception I received was from the London Stereoscopic Company which had a large premises occupying a corner of Regent Street. My enquiries were met with a suspicion which was almost hostile, and I went away with the impression that I must have unintentionally offended someone.

Despite this, I continued to wonder if there might be some businesses which were already using the lamps. My next task was to see if there was a photographic studio at any of the locations where Cloudsdale's papers might have been copied. These were Charing Cross and Stepney, and the two other stations on the route, Whitechapel and Fenchurch Street. My enquiries took me to all those places, and I discovered a number of photographic studios, each about five or ten minutes' walk from the nearest rail station. Whether or not there was time to carry out the photography of the documents was not relevant, since they all employed the light of the sun, which was sadly lacking on the day in question.

Ultimately, I was pleased that I had not troubled Holmes and Mycroft with the idea, and returned home wearier and wiser, to address myself to my studies.

I am often my own worst enemy, and following my unsuccessful enquiries, the arc lamp situation continued to prey on my mind until I was unable to stay silent on the subject. The next time I saw Holmes at Montague Street, I asked his permission to delve into his collection of newspapers, which were still in the process of being mined for articles of interest. I soon discovered an account of the demonstration of Jablochkoff candles at the West India Docks. Knowing that Holmes was more likely to take up my idea if he believed he had thought of it himself, I casually introduced it into our conversation. 'I saw these lamps in use when I was in Paris,' I said. 'They were very impressive.'

Holmes saw the possibilities at once. He took the paper from my hand and studied it intently. 'But as yet they have no commercial application elsewhere,' he observed.

After a brief struggle with my conscience, I finally admitted to my fruitless searches. Holmes listened to me with some amusement. 'You must tell Mycroft at our next meeting,' he said. 'He will have his own view on the matter.'

CHAPTER EIGHT

'Of course,' said Mycroft, casually, once Holmes had addressed him on the subject of arc lamps, 'that part of the story is now very apparent to me. As I am sure it is to you, also, Sherlock.'

I was quite rightly not admitted to that select company.

'Kindly enlighten us,' said Holmes.

'I have known for some time what must have happened. Only the means was uncertain, but now I am sure of it all,' Mycroft went on. 'It does not, unfortunately, clear Emmett from suspicion, although I remain confident that he was in no way involved.'

We were in his club at the time, in a private room with a decanter of fine sherry and a plate of excellent biscuits. To my surprise, Mycroft turned to address me directly. 'Stamford, you have been very useful, although you may not know it. I am indebted to you, for your observations and your investigation, which has saved my brother and me a great many hours of work. Your conclusions, while incorrect, have not been without interest. You have searched in vain for a photographic studio which employs electrical arc lamps. You have not found one since you have been told that none exist. That may not be the case. Not entirely. I think your unfriendly reception at the London Stereoscopic Company was because you were suspected of being a spy for a rival business. I am quite sure that they and most probably other leading studios are even now conducting tests of the use of these lamps in photography. All are hoping to be the first such business to make the announcement, which would be a considerable commercial advantage. You believed that your efforts were not of value. I disagree. It only now remains to locate the place where the copy was made, but for the moment I will act upon the belief that there is such a place to be found.'

Mycroft, who had a glass of sherry before him, selected a biscuit, and paused for refreshment. Neither I nor Holmes wished to interrupt him.

'We have been considering, given what we know of the character of Mr Cloudsdale, what means were used to induce him to part with the envelope of secret papers, even for a short time,' Mycroft continued, dabbing his lips with a napkin. 'Would he have given them up to a stranger? Not without some serious threats. And yet, when he arrived at his destination, he was not at that time a frightened man. He appeared merely to be unsettled and did his best to pass it off as due to the transport delay. The fact that he did not succeed confirms what I already believed: that he was not an accomplished liar. I must conclude therefore, that he gave the envelope to someone he knew and trusted. Someone senior in rank, who had the authority to demand it. I wonder what reason he was given for this unusual and unexpected interruption. If he was told he must be parted from the envelope for a few minutes only, he would have felt reassured that neither a photographic nor handwritten copy was possible in so short a time. He cannot have been permitted to observe the process. During those missing minutes, the envelope was opened, and the contents photographed. The envelope was then resealed and returned to Cloudsdale.'

This analysis was so detailed and convincing, I asked, 'Have you deduced where this took place?'

Mycroft produced a copy of *The Times* and pointed to a small article. 'You will see that on the day Mr Cloudsdale disappeared, Sir Crawford Yates was attending a luncheon of the British Mercantile Association, at the City Hotel in London Street. He delivered a speech. It so happens that London Street is a bare two minutes' walk from Fenchurch Street station. Sir Crawford is by reputation a pillar of government service, which to my mind means that any unwise, illegal, or foolish actions he may have committed have not yet been exposed. I am sure that his interview with me was a blatant attempt to sow seeds of doubt in my mind about Emmett. He knows that we are friends, and I must be his closest ally. If Yates could shake my belief in Emmett, it would deprive my friend of his best support, and divert attention from his own suspect activities.'

I thought it was something of a coincidence that both Yates and Cloudsdale were within a few steps of each other at the same date and time, but kept my silence, especially as Holmes was smiling and nodding approvingly at his brother's statement. 'And Mrs Cloudsdale told us that her husband had been kept very busy in the week before his disappearance,' he said.

'Precisely,' said Mycroft. 'It was not by chance that his journey to Stepney and Yates's luncheon took place on the same day. Yates was in a position to manoeuvre Cloudsdale's duties to ensure that. He knew the times of Cloudsdale's travel, and the man was known to be particular to the minute. I think Yates was able to slip away briefly to intercept Cloudsdale at the station and persuade him of some urgent reason why he needed to give up the envelope for a short while. Cloudsdale was instructed to explain his lateness at Stepney as due to a delay on the train.

'Yates then either directed or conducted Cloudsdale to the place concerned, and returned to the City Hotel before he was missed. His status and authority were sufficient to ensure Cloudsdale's compliance.'

'We still don't know the location, but your theory and the time available suggests it was within a short walking distance of either Fenchurch Street station or Stepney,' said Holmes.

'I agree,' said Mycroft. 'Mr Stamford has already made enquiries at photographers' businesses in those places. We must cast our nets wider.'

'But why make the attempt on Cloudsdale's life?' I asked. 'If he had done this once he would probably have been asked to do it again. He might have proved very useful.'

'Yes, he might, and that could well have been the plan, to employ him as an agent on a regular basis, but supposing he had made his concern apparent?' said Mycroft. 'Perhaps as he waited for the envelope to be handed back to him, he began to reflect on the unusual and irregular demands that had been made on him. He was beginning to have doubts about the proceeding. His natural caution came into play, and suspicions arose. Maybe he was wondering if he had been duped. That would explain his state of unrest. He might have wondered if Yates could be trusted, and if not, then his own position was an extremely serious one. Supposing, on the envelope being returned to him, which must have been something of a relief, he had made an unguarded comment, that he would report to his masters at Whitehall regarding the unexpected variation in his mission, before he undertook such an exercise again.'

'A fatal error,' said Holmes. 'It meant that Cloudsdale had become a danger, and criminals of that type eliminate dangers. One member of the gang must have followed him to where the papers were to be delivered, then watched and waited for him as he made his way back to Stepney station and attempted unsuccessfully to push him under a carriage. Cloudsdale was able to board the train, and his pursuer, hampered by the crowds, did not.'

'But where is he?' I asked, hoping that the brothers had extended their deliberations to reach a conclusion.

'We can only hope that Cloudsdale was able to reach a place of safety,' said Holmes. 'However, his failure to communicate with his family is troubling. I agree that Yates must have been involved. He may even be the director of the gang, taking the profits while others did the hard work. But it will be hard to prove our conclusions until we have the rest of the gang in custody, when they will hopefully turn on him, and give him up to the authorities in order to reduce their sentences. Only then may we learn the true fate of Mr Cloudsdale.'

'But now let us consider the fact that we believe that the papers could have been copied by photography,' said Mycroft. 'Either that or some other scientific advance of which we as yet have no knowledge. Remember when I asked some of the senior men at Whitehall how we would know if the papers had fallen into enemy hands? I was simply told that it would be evident, but more than that they would not divulge. The recent explosion in the Baltic and the reaction to this event in government circles rather suggests that the plans were put into effect. If that is the case, we should now consider why the test of the new steerable torpedo failed so badly?'

'Perhaps there was a mistake in the plans?' I suggested.

Mycroft made a note on a paper. 'Theory number one.'

'The plans were correct, but an error was made by the thieves when putting them into practice,' said Holmes.

'Two,' said Mycroft.

'The plans were correct, but the quality of the copy was poor, which led to an error,' I said.

'Three,' said Mycroft.

'The plans were correct, but they would never have worked,' said Holmes.

'Four.' Mycroft smiled. 'What a world of excellent theories we have here. And I would like to add another. The plans carried by Mr Cloudsdale were quite deliberately incomplete, either that or there was an error placed there on purpose. This was to ensure that if they were to fall into unfriendly hands, they would be useless. One small additional piece of information, or one apparently trivial correction was required. That information would be transmitted by another method. It could have been as simple as a number and communicated by word of mouth at the point of delivery. The recipients of the pictures would not have had that information. It was so subtle a difference that they might not initially have realised anything was missing.'

'Is your suggestion a technique often used for government papers?' I asked.

'That is only known for certain by men whose salaries are considerably greater than mine,' said Mycroft, with a smile. 'But we should bear it in mind. I believe we still think there is a possibility that Cloudsdale is alive and in hiding. But once the men who copied the papers suspect that there is additional material required, they will stop at nothing to find Cloudsdale and try and extract from him what they need. An experience he is unlikely to survive.'

CHAPTER NINE

I had spent a considerable amount of time on the case so far, and after this meeting, plunged with renewed urgency into my medical studies. My final examinations leading to my qualifying as a surgeon were to take place in the following year, and I am not one of those students who leave this essential preparation to the last minute. Even had there been no examinations to spur my efforts, I would still have devoted significant time to my books and practical work. In my youthful employment as surgical dresser to John Watson, I had never imagined that the career of surgeon could ever be mine. I would have failed my esteemed mentor if I had not tried to become the best surgeon I could possibly be.

Holmes had passed the results of our deliberations to Sergeant Lestrade, and on learning that the papers could have been photographed at an unknown location, the police now had another search on their hands. As I worked, I waited, occasionally distracted in my mind by the hope of receiving news of Mr Cloudsdale. I was now convinced that he was an honest man whose dedication had been used against him and embroiling him in a situation for which he was wholly unprepared.

Two days passed without news. I was at a table in the college library, so deep in study that I did not even hear the approach of Holmes, who tapped me lightly on the shoulder and beckoned me to go with him. His expression was such that I knew this would not be a brief interview, and I gathered my papers and took them with me.

'Lestrade is waiting for us,' said Holmes as soon as we were in a place where we could talk without being overheard. 'It seems that the torso of a man has been found in the Thames.'

I did not ask if his brother would join us. I thought this was one occasion when Mycroft would not be disappointed at his lack of involvement in a meeting.

Lestrade was in the entrance hall of the college, pacing about impatiently. He nodded brusquely as we approached and motioned us to accompany him outside to where a cab was waiting. 'Millbank Street,' he told the driver, and we leapt in.

'I am hoping this find does not prove to be Cloudsdale,' he said, as the cab rattled away. 'All we have so far is a torso, but it is that of an adult male, and he has probably been dead for a few weeks. There are other reports of missing men of course, but these are often older, and less well nourished. But I hope we can identify him one way or another.'

'Where was it found?' asked Holmes.

'Under the arch of Lambeth Bridge, on the west shore of the river,' said Lestrade. 'It had sunk into the mud. It was reported by a boatman, and both he and the river police are sure it can't have been there long, or they would have seen it before now. Lambeth is a footbridge only, so the torso might have been carried to the spot and dropped there at night.'

'Have you seen it?' I asked.

'Not yet,' said Lestrade grimly. 'But when I have had that pleasure, I have to report to Chief Inspector Foinette if I think it's our man. Oh, and no luck on photographers so far,' he added. 'None of them are advertising that they are using these new electric lamps, which would be all over the papers if they had them. But we are keeping alert in case we hear more.'

'Do you think there is still a possibility that Mr Cloudsdale will be found alive?' I asked.

'If he is, he should have found some way of communicating with his wife by now,' said Lestrade. 'Not that she would tell us if he had. We have been keeping watch for notes delivered to her, and any unusual visits she has made, but there has been nothing to suggest that she knows more than she is saying. This find may settle the question.'

'Why are we going to Millbank Street?' I asked as we passed the looming grandeur of the Houses of Parliament as we travelled in the direction of the notorious penitentiary.

'It turns out that the Westminster coroner doesn't like rotting corpses being taken out of the river and stretchered halfway across London, for want of a proper mortuary, so there's a new one. Not much of one, but it's better than nothing.'

'I would first of all like to go and see where the remains were found,' said Holmes. 'Were they examined by a medical man in place?'

'No. I think the boatman who found the torso took the view that he didn't need a doctor to tell him the man was dead and fetched the nearest constable.'

Holmes grunted in annoyance.

'Oh, and we have another report of a possible sighting of Cloudsdale on the day he disappeared,' added Lestrade. 'A gentleman on the Charing Cross service saw a man board the train at Fenchurch Street who was perspiring and looked either tired or upset. The date and time are a good fit. The witness left the train at Whitechapel, but the man continued the journey. Cloudsdale may have made it back to Charing Cross after all.'

We spent a little time at the bridge. The waters had risen since the remains were retrieved, so the precise location of the torso had been covered, together with any clues that might possibly have still been visible.

'Do you have any evidence to show for certain where the torso was initially placed in the river?' Holmes asked.

'No, none so far,' said Lestrade. 'We have constables out searching the banks and asking questions. Someone disposing of an entire corpse might have attracted some attention, but it's less likely with a package the size of a torso.'

There was a set of steps leading down from the bridge to the shoreline, and Holmes made all of us muddy our shoes before he concluded that the disposal could easily have been made at that very spot without anyone observing it. 'How it was done, either by road or the shoreline it is impossible to say,' he said. 'The location might have been chosen quite deliberately to confuse the issue. Perhaps it was.'

We mounted the steps to street level.

My younger readers may well be shocked to learn of the lack of public mortuaries in London in the 1870s. When someone died at home, the corpse would remain there for as long as it took to arrange a burial, which in view of the cost to poorer households, might take some while. Families who ate and slept in a single room were frequently obliged to share their only living space with the dead for a week or two, or even longer. For unidentified remains there were no formal arrangements. In 1873, sections of a body were disposed of by a murderer at ten different locations along the river Thames from Battersea to Limehouse, and the unclaimed fragments had been taken to nearby workhouses or police stations. When it was suspected that they might all be parts of one woman, they were gathered at the Clapham and Wandsworth workhouse. There, under the direction of police surgeon Thomas Bond, the point was proved by sewing them together.

The torso found under Lambeth Bridge in 1877 did not fare much better. It had been wrapped roughly in fabric and tied about with cord. A brief examination by the constable called to the scene revealed decomposing flesh and an unmistakeable stench. The remains were loaded onto a handcart and transported to the nearest building able and willing to receive it, a small brick outhouse at the rear of some shops in Millbank Street. It had not been built to receive corpses, but resembled a storehouse pressed into a use for which it had never been intended. Anything less like a proper mortuary could not be imagined, although it did continue to be used as such for quite a number of years. The primary essentials for any mortuary are adequate light and ventilation, and proper sanitary arrangements. The surgeon has not only to examine the remains, but he must also collect samples in clean containers for further analysis, and display bodies respectfully for identification. None of these features existed at Millbank Street. Even basic materials such as towels had to be provided by the surgeon. I was, however, extremely eager to see the remains, since they were being examined by Thomas Bond himself, and I looked forward to meeting him.

CHAPTER TEN

The mortuary was guarded by a constable, who looked perfectly content to be outside in the fresh air. He opened the door to admit us to the cold and damp interior, where we found Surgeon Bond at work. Bond was then thirty-six years of age, a serious-looking man with a luxuriant moustache. He was doing his best in trying circumstances, having been provided with a table on which to place the remains, and another to accommodate his tools and any evidence. An oil lamp was the sole illumination, and sanitation was provided by a basin, a piece of carbolic soap and a jug of water. The odour of the soap did little to allay the foul reek of decomposition which filled the little space with its tiny windows so thickly it was almost tangible.

Although Bond had not previously met Holmes, it was obvious from his greeting that my friend's name was known to him, through his contribution to the solution of recent crimes, and Bond was happy to allow us to view the remains and offer any suggestions.

There was little enough to see. The torso was undoubtedly that of a human male, but the head was missing, as were the arms, and the body had been severed at the waist. I saw at once that the dismemberment had not been carried out by a surgeon, at least not a sober one, but neither was it the ragged efforts of an amateur driven by desperation to attempt this task for the first time. The discolouration and friable texture of the skin suggested that death had not been recent. There was no obvious indication of cause of death, although the simple facts of mutilation and disposal inevitably suggested murder.

'Well-nourished,' said Bond, 'age — hard to estimate — anywhere between thirty and sixty. No obvious distinguishing marks. He must have been of good muscular development. The cuts are cleanly made, not by a surgeon, but someone used to this kind of work, a butcher perhaps. I would estimate that he has been dead for some three to five weeks, but very little of that time has been spent immersed in water. There is evidence of an early infestation which would only have taken place in the air. But I feel that the remains must have been held for a time in a closed container which would have somewhat retarded decay and were brought to the Thameside only recently. Decomposition has advanced very rapidly following exposure to air. The remains would have been able to float, but in the absence of any sightings I am inclined to think they were not dropped into moving water but directly into the shallows and stagnant mud where they were found. I will take a sample of the stomach contents, but I doubt that it will be possible to identify his last meal. The best means of discovering his identity would be reports of missing persons and also the material found wrapping the remains, which is a shirt. Bodies disposed of in this manner tend to be wrapped in whatever comes to hand, and the deceased's clothing is often pressed into use. The body must first have been stripped for easier dismemberment, then the torso wrapped and tied with common twine.' He gestured to the other table and Holmes went to look at the muddied shirt and the cord.

'The shirt is inside out,' observed Holmes. 'I agree that it was stripped from the body after death.' He studied it carefully. 'There is a maker's label, and the material is of good quality. This is a business shirt, not one worn by a labouring man. If you would permit me to restore it right side out?'

'Please do,' said Bond. 'Lay it out and we will take a closer look.'

Holmes carefully handled the badly soiled item, examining the cuffs with particular attention. 'There is a small ink-stain on the left cuff, which is a little more worn than the right. The man must be left-handed. It is the type usually fastened by a cufflink, which is missing. And the right cuff — halloa — what is this?' Trapped in the fold between cuff and sleeve we saw a single cufflink. Surgeon Bond brought the lamp to bear on it. It was gold, oval with a beaded edge. We searched minutely through all the fabric of the shirt, but the second cufflink was not to be found.

'It is possible,' said Bond, 'that the murderer, having removed both cufflinks in order to pull the shirt from the body, dropped this one as he carried out the wrapping. His carelessness could be the key to identifying the remains.'

'Might it lead us to the killer if you found the other one?' I asked, hopefully.

'By now it might have been sold for the weight of the gold,' said Lestrade. 'But even if we knew the seller, he would just claim he had found it in the street.'

Holmes was examining the cord that had bound the shirt around the torso. The knots were intact as Bond had been careful not to untie them but had cut the cord with his penknife. 'The study of knots is an important one for the solution of crime,' said Holmes. 'Some will instantly identify the profession of the man who tied them. These are not sailor's knots, but are carefully done, efficient, perhaps by a tradesman used to parcelling goods.'

'I fear,' said Bond, 'that unless the head is discovered or poison found, the cause of death may remain a mystery. There is a small mark just under the left armpit, which may be an old scar or scratch, or just a skin fold. It's hard to tell. Either way I don't think it contributed to his death.'

'I am hoping the other body parts will be found,' said Lestrade. 'Of course, they might have been weighted down.'

'I see no signs on this cord that any attempt has been made to weight the torso,' said Holmes.

'I would not necessarily expect it,' said Bond. 'The river is not the best place to make a body disappear, even quite small parts were discovered in the Battersea case. No, I sometimes think that killers who throw body parts in the river or on the shoreline are not trying to hide them. It is almost a form of display. A demonstration of their power. They take pride in their work.'

Shocking as this observation was, I could see his point, but wondered what kind of man would do such a dreadful thing. Perhaps, I thought, a man whose mind had given way from drink or a disease of the brain. It was a conundrum for men more expert in these matters than I.

'What do you say concerning the possibility that this is the body of Mr Cloudsdale?' asked Lestrade. 'He is — or was — a government servant who was last seen more than four weeks ago. You say the deceased was of good muscular development and we know that Cloudsdale attended a gymnasium.'

'I see nothing here to rule that out as an identification,' said Bond. 'His family should be shown the shirt and cufflink. They may wish to see the remains as well. I would not deny them if they insist. In the meantime, I will have the torso preserved in spirits of wine pending inspection by the coroner's jury and final identification.'

As Surgeon Bond cleansed his dissection tools in the basin of soapy water we heard raised voices outside, the constable, his tones firm and appeasing, and a much louder female sound like the bark of an angry mastiff.

'I think the news has got about,' said Bond, with a smile. 'The body will soon be declared to be that of every missing husband in the vicinity.'

The constable peered in. 'There is a — a lady here,' he said, his voice slightly muffled by the kerchief clutched over his nose. 'Very insistent. I've told her it's not a pretty sight.'

'Never mind that!' said a substantial woman, roughly elbowing the young policeman out of the way. 'My father is a butcher and I've seen it all!'

She wore a greasy-looking gown, the sleeves rolled to her elbows revealing muscular forearms and roughened red hands. There was a stout cloth apron tied about her waist, a heavy shawl around her shoulders, and a dusty bonnet on her head, doing its best to frame a square face with heavy features. She brought with her a powerful odour of beef intestines, vinegar, and perspiration.

'If you wish to view the remains, I have no objection,' said Bond. 'Kindly let me know your name and that of any person who is missing?'

'Collett,' said the woman. 'And I have not seen my husband for the best part of a month.'

'I am sorry to say all that has been found is a portion of a body, the torso,' said Bond, stepping aside, so she could see what lay on the table. 'Are there any marks which might distinguish him?'

'Well, if you had his arms there would be tattoos, and he had a bad foot which I would know straight away was his.' She stepped forward to gaze more closely at the remains, which she did without flinching. 'This one has been dead awhile,' she said.

'When did you last see your husband?' asked Lestrade.

'Three weeks last Friday. He gets his wages then and doesn't come home till late. But that day he didn't come home at all. No one's seen him. I thought he had fallen down drunk somewhere. Went into the river and drowned. I used to tell him, "You'll fall in and drown one day, the state you come home in!" Did this one drown?'

'That is one line of enquiry, but I will know more after a full examination,' said Bond. 'What work did your husband do?'

'Warehouseman.'

'Heavy labour, then. What was he wearing when you last saw him?'

'Work shirt, trousers, boots. Overcoat.'

'Did he breakfast before he went to work?'

'Yes, he had a plate of herrings and bread. I gave him a packet of tripe to take with him. He likes tripe.'

'The torso was wrapped in a shirt,' said Lestrade. 'Can you identify it as something your husband might have worn or owned?'

Mrs Collett stared at the shirt. Though marked with dirt, blood, and fluids of decomposition, it was clearly of good quality. 'No,' she admitted, 'but that doesn't mean anything. It might have come from anywhere.' She looked closely at the torso again. 'Yes, that's him alright. I mean, I ought to know my own husband, oughtn't I?'

'Of course,' said Bond, kindly.

'What about this?' said Lestrade, showing her the cufflink. 'Have you seen this before?'

'If you're trying to play a trick on me that won't work,' she said.

'Have you ever seen this?' repeated Lestrade.

'No, I haven't, but if you find the head, let me know. There's a bit of one ear missing, he lost it in a fight.'

'Give the constable your address and we will let you know if any more remains are found, as well as the date and place of the inquest,' said Lestrade. He wrapped the cufflink in his handkerchief and put it in his pocket.

'Will I get a certificate?' she demanded. 'I'll need a death certificate for the burial club.'

'If the inquest confirms the identification,' said Lestrade.

'You'll see me again,' she promised, then grunted and left.

'Not all widows are stricken with grief,' said Bond.

'I'd like to know how much she has him insured for,' said Lestrade. 'Might have poisoned him for the money. He could be in any number of burial clubs.'

'If it is he,' observed Holmes. 'Mrs Cloudsdale might think differently.'

CHAPTER ELEVEN

The inquest on the torso found in the river was to open the following day in the boardroom of the vestry hall, in Mount Street, near Grosvenor Square. No further remains had been found to assist identification, and the pickled torso, having been placed in a shell for transport, was residing in the mortuary of the nearby workhouse, waiting to be viewed by the coroner's jury.

My heart went out to Mrs Cloudsdale who arrived leaning heavily on the arm of a youth who, having previously seen his photograph, I knew was the eldest son, returned from Cambridge to comfort her. They were accompanied by a lady of similar age, who meandered peering myopically about the courtroom. I felt confident that this was the short-sighted cousin Hilda. Once Mrs Cloudsdale was seated, the youth obligingly manoeuvred cousin Hilda into place. The family was not yet in mourning, but all were dressed in their darkest attire and Mrs Cloudsdale was as thickly veiled as any widow.

Mrs Collett, arriving clad as we had seen her the day before, was alone. She waited with a surly expression, her arms folded, ready to deal with all arguments that might arise, and start one herself if required.

Men of the press, who always saw the potential for a good story in a dismembered corpse, were there in abundance with notebooks and pencils, and there were the usual persons who had come in out of the cold, and were huddled at the back, like theatregoers in the cheap seats.

The coroner, Mr Bedford, opened the proceedings saying that he hoped even if it was not yet possible to determine cause of death, that the remains might be identified. We first heard from the boatman who had found the torso, the policeman who had been summoned, and the river police, all of whom were certain it had not been there during the preceding few days.

Inspector Foinette told the court that there was no evidence to prove conclusively exactly where and when the torso had been placed in the Thames. Careful searches were still being undertaken for more body parts, but nothing further had been found.

Surgeon Bond was next called to give evidence. He told the court that he was conducting further tests, but he did not think he would be able to show conclusively what the deceased's last meal had been. He had not been able to detect any trace of common poisons or soporific drugs. He was unable at present to arrive at a cause of death, although he had ruled out drowning. The torso was that of an adult male, well-nourished. There were no obvious features which would help identification. There was a small mark or skin fold which could have been produced by decomposition. He showed the court the shirt and twine that had bound the torso, which were laid out on the evidence table. Sergeant Lestrade then appeared from the back of the court, bringing the cufflink which he placed very carefully and deliberately beside the shirt. He turned and eyed the rabble of attendees with a warning expression, then stood nearby keeping a steady watch on the little gold oval.

Young Gregory Cloudsdale was next to give evidence. He was very quietly spoken but maintained his dignity and composure. He said that he had viewed the torso, as his mother was too unwell to do so. He could not positively say if it was the body of his father but saw no reason it could not be. He thought the cufflink was his father's.

When Mrs Cloudsdale's name was called, she began to shake. Her son took her hand and helped her rise to her feet and walk slowly to the chair near to the coroner's table. The watchers in court appeared to be holding their breath in case the unhappy woman suddenly fell to the floor, but she was able to reach the seat in safety. Mr Bedford signalled to one of his officers, who provided the witness with a glass of water. The pressmen scribbled rapidly. If there was no actual drama then they could always report on the demeanour of the lady, wringing every last drop of pathos from her plight.

The coroner waited patiently until he felt the witness was ready to answer questions and spoke to her with great kindness. Since she had not viewed the torso, he asked her only about the shirt and the cufflink. Mrs Cloudsdale said she was certain that both were her husband's. The shirt was the kind he usually wore to the office. He had several others in his wardrobe, and they were the same style and size. He was left-handed and she had previously noticed the ink stain on the left cuff and tried her best to remove it. She was quite certain that it was the same stain. The cufflink was also his. It was one of a pair that had belonged to his late father. If the other was ever found, she would know it at once by a slight fault in one part of the beaded edge.

She was asked no more questions, and her son came forward to conduct her back to her place.

The next witness called was Mrs Sarah Collett, who strode to her seat with energy, sank into it as if she owned it, and stared fearlessly about the courtroom. Mr Bedford had just opened his mouth to speak when she announced, 'Well, I've heard what's been said here, and it's all nonsense and hogwash!'

'And why is that, Mrs Collett?' asked the coroner, politely.

'Because the body which I have seen with my own eyes, and my sympathy to the lady but she never saw it, that body is my husband, Dickie, or what's left of him. If you had even one arm it would be clear as day, what with his tattoos.'

'Can you say what makes you so certain of that identification?' asked Mr Bedford.

'It's the scar on his left side. Just here.' She prodded a rib just below her arm. 'It's from an old knife wound. I know that because I gave it him.'

An inquest is rarely a place for amusement, but I saw several of the observers making strenuous efforts not to smile, and the pressmen scribbled faster than before.

'You stabbed your husband?' asked the coroner, in astonishment.

'It was nothing, just a little love tap. We had our arguments, all people do.'

'I see,' said Bedford. He glanced at Lestrade, who appeared disinclined to take Mrs Collett into custody. 'You have heard Surgeon Bond tell the court that he thought the mark might have been a scratch or just a skin fold, as it was hard to determine exactly what it was.'

'I heard, but I don't believe it,' said Mrs Collett firmly. 'He doesn't know, but I do. You think I don't know my own husband? I washed him down when he was too ill or drunk to wash himself, which I'm sure fine ladies don't do for their menfolk.' There followed some further comments I am sure my readers would not wish me to record here, regarding her familiarity with her husband's form. One lady sitting at the back, rose, and very pointedly left the room.

'What is your husband's age and occupation?' asked the coroner, in an effort to turn the subject of conversation.

'Forty-seven. Labourer in a furniture warehouse at Bermondsey docks. And I didn't see all the police going about trying to find him like they have been doing for Mr Cloudsdale. No, when I went and told them my husband hadn't been home, they just said he must have been drunk and laid down to sleep it off, and he would turn up soon. Said they would keep an eye out for him, but I don't think they ever did.'

'And you last saw him, when?'

'Last month. Friday the fifth.'

The coroner glanced at his notes. 'The last time Mr Cloudsdale was seen was the previous Monday. Is your husband insured?'

'Burial club, fourpence a week. It won't be much, if that what you're thinking. He was a good man for all his faults. Worth more alive than dead, which is a lot more than you can say of some husbands.' She looked around the room, pointing a stubby finger, as if many of the men present fell into that inferior category.

'Thank you, Mrs Collett, I have no further questions.'

She leaned towards the coroner and thumped his desk with her fist. 'Well, I have! I want to know when I can bury my husband, or what's left of him!'

'It may not be possible to answer your question today,' said Bedford, gently. Mrs Collett snorted angrily and returned to her seat.

Mr Bedford addressed the jury. 'I propose to adjourn the proceedings for one week to enable Surgeon Bond to complete his tests. I shall not at this juncture be asking for a determination of cause of death. Can you advise me if you are satisfied as to the identity of the remains?'

There was a hurried consultation amongst the jurymen, then the foreman rose. 'Mr coroner, sir, based on the identification of the shirt and cufflink by Mrs Cloudsdale, which are very convincing indeed, we are content to identify the remains as those of Mr Anthony Cloudsdale.'

'Very well, that is so noted,' said Mr Bedford.

Mrs Collett rose, and I thought she was about to make an angry remark, but instead she paused at the sound of Mrs Cloudsdale dissolving into sobs. She nodded, the silent recognition by a wife of the loss suffered by another wife, then she left the room without a word.

Holmes and Mycroft said nothing, but they were thoughtful, and I assumed they would communicate their deliberations in due course. I suspected that nothing could be achieved until more body parts were discovered, either that or Surgeon Bond's microscope revealed something that threw new light on the mystery. But as the days passed, there was no more news, and all remained in darkness.

CHAPTER TWELVE

'I have recently discovered something which has unsettled me,' said Mycroft when we next met at his club. 'When the inquest delivered its verdict, I considered what actions the gang must have taken in the days following the disappearance of the unfortunate Mr Cloudsdale.'

'You believe the torso is his?' asked Holmes. 'I am not at all convinced of it.'

'Whether or not it is his, I think the man is not alive,' said Mycroft. 'But the enquiries made by the police at Whitehall have concentrated thus far on the men who were there or not on the day Cloudsdale disappeared, and their alibis for that time. If efforts were made thereafter, perhaps to secure the man, question him, extract information, and then dispose of him, we ought to be looking at the days that followed, quite possibly the whole week. I therefore returned to my research at Whitehall, which was not a trivial procedure I can assure you, given the number of men who work there and the period covered. Also, as I am sure you understand, I have to be very careful when asking questions. I must investigate without giving any hint that that is what I am doing. As you know, I suspect Yates. I still suspect Yates, but I now think that after he inveigled Cloudsdale to give up the envelope his work was done. He has led an exemplary existence ever since. Quite deliberately, I am sure. But everything I have learned about him suggests to me that he is not a great intellect, and I do not think he is the author of the plan.'

'I am increasingly sure that there is a large gang, perhaps larger than we have previously imagined, each member of which has a separate task to perform,' said Holmes.

'I agree. And it was not sufficient for me to just look at which men were at their desks during their normal working hours. In the days following Cloudsdale's disappearance, they might have been nefariously occupied after their workaday was done. I confess, I was not sure exactly what it was that I was looking for. And then — I found something.' He sighed. 'And to be truthful, I wish I had not.'

'Does this involve Emmett? asked Holmes.

'Yes. Interviews were being conducted at Whitehall for several days after Cloudsdale was reported missing, on the Monday. Emmett has told us he had been interviewed by the police twice. The first occasion was two days later, on the Wednesday, when, the honest fellow that he is, he mentioned receiving the fifty-pound note, which he thought might have come from his relative, Guthrie. He tried to trace Guthrie but without success and has only recently been told that Guthrie is dead. He says that his mother did not tell him his cousin had died, in fact she never mentioned him at all, which he attributes to her sense of shame at having a relative in prison. The second time he was questioned was about ten days later, when a constable came to ask him if he had established where the money had come from. He has not and remains in the dark. I am not sure how seriously the police regarded this incident as he had been so open about it.

'I have now discovered that on the Tuesday, the day after Cloudsdale went missing, Emmett went to his supervisor Mr Leslie, saying he had been called away to a meeting. He asked permission to leave early, at half past four, promising to make up the time later. Mr Leslie, whom I have not spoken to, might have assumed it was in connection with the enquiry about Cloudsdale, perhaps an interview with the police, and gave his permission without quibble. But it was not. Sherlock, I have to thank you for your efforts in obtaining the crucial information from Lestrade. He is a valuable ally. Emmett has so far been interviewed twice, but not on that Tuesday.

'But, I asked myself, what was this meeting to which Emmett had been called the day after Cloudsdale vanished? Why had he not mentioned it to the police or, as far as I am aware, to anyone else other than seeking permission to leave early from Mr Leslie? Was there indeed a meeting of any kind? I have been able through a little surreptitious sleight of hand, to examine the time schedules of all his colleagues in the administrative departments. All were either at their desks until five o'clock at least, some even later, or on leave, with their absence fully explained.'

'Then we must speak to Emmett,' said Holmes.

'I have just done so,' said Mycroft. 'When I raised the subject, he became somewhat disturbed. He said that there was a meeting, but it had nothing to do with the police or Cloudsdale. It was related to his work. He assured me that he had done nothing unlawful, and I believe him. It was with some difficulty that I was able to persuade him he ought to speak to you. I promised him absolute confidentiality unless he gave us his permission to disclose it elsewhere. That is why I proposed we see him here. He might have brought Miss Jessup with him if we had met in the tea shop. I felt he might speak more openly if Miss Jessup was not with us.'

'That is very wise,' said Holmes.

Mycroft glanced at his watch. 'He must be waiting in the foyer now,' he said. 'I shall ask for him to be admitted and sent up.'

When Emmett arrived, he was pale and making a valiant effort to control a simmering anxiety. He sat at the table and Mycroft asked for coffee to be sent. I thought Emmett looked in need of something stronger but did not say so. 'I assure you gentlemen,' he said when he had refreshed himself, 'I have nothing to hide except what is required of me by my profession.'

'Tell us what you can about the Tuesday, the day immediately after Mr Cloudsdale disappeared, when you left the office half an hour early,' said Mycroft. 'You have already told me you were not being interviewed by the police.'

'On my honour it was nothing to do with that sad business,' said Emmett. 'No, it was something else. It related to my work. I was called to a meeting. I sent a note to my mother to say that I was working late that day. She will confirm that.'

'What time did you arrive home?' asked Holmes.

'It was before seven, about a quarter to, I think. Yes, we dined at seven.'

'I appreciate that our work can sometimes be of a sensitive nature,' said Mycroft. 'There may be confidential matters which you are not to disclose outside the service. It would, however, be as well to ensure that if you are ever questioned on the subject of your absence that day, you would be able at the very least to provide proof of where you were and with whom.'

Emmett looked flustered. 'I don't think —' he began and stopped.

'Are you able to name a colleague who was at the same meeting?'

'I cannot,' said Emmett.

'I am glad you have not done so,' said Mycroft. 'Since it reassures me that you are being truthful. I am aware that no other men left early that day. Emmett, please, be frank with us. If nothing else, just say where you were.'

Emmett shook his head. 'Even if I did, I am not sure it would help,' he said.

'I am sorry to say this,' said Mycroft, more sternly, 'but I am obliged to ask if there is a woman in the case. If that is so, you would disappoint me, but only a little. Many men, when approaching marriage, feel that they should fully complete their education in worldly matters before plighting their troth to their beloved.'

'I — no, nothing of the sort!' exclaimed Emmett, visibly shocked at Mycroft's indelicate suggestion. 'There is no woman at all involved in this. It was official government business. A meeting of significant importance which I was ordered not to divulge to anyone!'

'If that is the case, I would certainly not require you to reveal what was discussed at the meeting,' said Holmes. 'But I would at least like to know where it took place. If necessary, you should request permission from at least one other person who was present, to provide us with the address, and who is willing to support what you have just told us.'

'I can't,' said Emmett, miserably.

Mycroft leaned forward intently. 'Emmett, I beg of you, be sensible,' he urged. 'Imagine how this will look if the police were to hear of it, and I am sure that they will. They must even now be extending their investigation to the period after Cloudsdale vanished, and Mr Leslie has a note of your absence. Your silence on the subject will look very strange to them. I know you are an honest man, and you should have nothing to fear if you tell the truth. If there are sensitive issues involved which cannot be made public, then I am sure some senior man will vouch for you. Now then, are you at least prepared to say who invited you to the meeting?'

'It was on official notepaper,' said Emmett. 'The kind we use for internal memoranda. I was told to attend a meeting at a certain place and time for a briefing on matters of great importance which would be revealed when I arrived. Only the very highest levels knew of it. I was to tell no-one about it unless they mentioned it to me first.'

'The signature?'

'It was not a name but on behalf of a committee. A department. International Communications.'

'I do not know of such a department,' said Mycroft. 'Do you still have this paper?'

'No, I had to take it with me to obtain admission.'

'And you went to this meeting?'

'Yes.'

'Please, without naming names or revealing secrets, tell us what happened.'

At length, Emmett spoke. 'I — went to the address. It was in Bayswater and appeared to be an ordinary house. I had been told to ring the bell for one of the apartments. Apartment number two. The door was opened by a young man — a valet, I think. I had never seen him before, and he did not give his name. But he said that I was expected; in fact, he knew my name.

'He asked to see the invitation and I gave it to him. He looked at it, put it in his pocket and said that he would conduct me to where the meeting would take place.

'We went upstairs to the next floor. On the way he said that the other gentlemen expected were not yet there, but I should go in and wait for them. He unlocked the door and let me in. It was a plainly furnished room. There was a desk, with paper, pen and ink, and some chairs gathered about. There were other rooms in the apartment, but I didn't enter them.

'The valet said that while I waited, I should sit at the desk and write an essay on what I considered to be the principal points of importance in the way that official meetings were conducted. I gathered from him that my thoughts and contribution to the discussion would be greatly appreciated.

'I sat down and began. I don't know how long I took over the essay. I supposed it was a test of some kind, to assess my suitability for an important position. To see if I was capable of clear thinking. Naturally, I gave the questions a great deal of thought, and took care over the task.

'Once I had completed the essay, I continued to wait. I didn't want to leave as I had been told that the meeting was important. Also, I thought that the period of waiting might be a part of the test. I think I must have been there in all for about an hour.

'Then, just as I thought I ought to see if I could find the valet again, he appeared. He told me that the other gentlemen had unexpectedly been prevented from attending, but they had sent him a note saying that the subject matter was of such importance that the meeting would have to be held very soon, and I was to await instructions. He said I should leave. And naturally, I did. I went home.'

'And did you hear any more?' asked Holmes.

'No, nothing.'

'You didn't mention it to another person?'

'No, I was told not to. And no-one else has said anything on the subject to me.'

'What an extraordinary business,' said Mycroft. 'Emmett, I want you to think very carefully. When you returned to your desk the next morning, was there anything amiss? Had anything been taken, or altered? Was there any sign that your papers had been moved?'

'No, it was all as I had left it,' said Emmett. 'I keep my work very tidy. And I can assure you, there was nothing of a sensitive nature on or in my desk.'

'It was a complicated charade merely to obtain access to Emmett's desk for that short time,' said Holmes. 'If that was all they wanted they could have simply waited until he left at five o'clock as usual.'

Emmett looked bewildered. It took time, but eventually he understood what Holmes was suggesting. 'Then you think — you think there was no such meeting? That it was all some sort of ruse?'

'Unless we hear to the contrary, that is what I think,' said Holmes.

Emmett was struggling with this statement. 'If that is true then I have been very foolish,' he said. 'But now you say it — now I look at it — yes, that is a possible explanation. But I swear to you, all I did was go to the place and wait there and write an essay and then I went home. I cannot see that any harm has been done. Perhaps it was all a misunderstanding? A joke?'

'We should pay a visit,' said Holmes. 'Bayswater, you say?'

'Yes — we must go there at once,' said Emmett. 'I want to speak to that valet and have him tell me what game he was playing and for whom.'

'We are at your disposal,' said Mycroft.

'If you are right, I am ashamed to have been taken in like that, but what else was I to do?' said Emmett. 'I believe in doing my duty and obeying my superiors — and it was official memorandum paper, I am sure of that. I don't know, I don't understand it at all. Well, come with me, and I will show you the way. At least I can remember the address.'

CHAPTER THIRTEEN

We hired a four-wheeler to take us to the location. Our way lay west, some three or four miles, along St James's, Piccadilly, skirting Hyde Park, onto Bayswater Road, then into the well-lit streets of long terraces, in one of which we alighted. These were respectable-looking houses, three storeys in height, and all very well kept. They had been built for substantial families and their servants, but many had been divided into smaller residences, fashionable apartments each occupying the whole of one floor, and rented out at good prices. I thought this impressive facade had a great deal to do with the success of whatever trick had been played on Emmett. He must have been wholly convinced of the importance of this supposed meeting. Although the houses were modelled according to the same design, our companion appeared confident as he led us to the house in question.

'This is the one,' he said. 'I remember the number and the little stone lions on either side of the door. And see the bells, marked 1, 2, 3, and Housekeeper.' He pressed the bell for apartment number two.

'The only person you saw that day was the valet,' said Holmes. 'Can you provide us with a description of him?'

'He was young, about twenty I would say. Clean shaven. Not tall, but active looking. And I thought — well, somehow it crossed my mind that he might have once been a sailor.'

'What made you think that?' asked Mycroft.

Emmett gave this some thought. 'Yes, I recall now, it was when we entered the room and he turned and spoke to me. It was the only time I saw him close up and I noticed that his ears were pierced. I know that sailors do that, or gypsies.'

'That is something at least,' said Holmes.

We waited impatiently for several minutes, but no-one came to the door. 'I suggest we speak to the housekeeper,' said Holmes, and she was duly summoned.

The door was opened by a maid. 'Good evening, sirs,' she said. 'If you are come about an apartment the housekeeper has told me to say that they are all taken.'

'We wish to pay a visit to the occupant of apartment two, but there is no answer to the bell,' said Holmes. 'Do you know when the tenant will return?'

'That I can't say, sir. The lady has been abroad for more than four weeks, but she still has the tenancy of the apartment.'

'A lady?' exclaimed Emmett, incredulously.

The maid, startled by his tone, fixed him with a firm look. 'Yes, sir, a lady, and her maid. Very respectable, as are all our tenants.'

'I see,' said Holmes. 'Well, that does explain why there is no answer. May I ask if there is a young gentleman here, about twenty years of age, a valet, to whom we might speak?'

'There is no-one living in this house of that description, sir.'

'But there must be!' Emmett interposed. 'I was here at this very house on the second of last month, and I rang the bell for apartment two and he opened the door and let me in. He had the key to the apartment.'

The maid's expression softened into a look she probably reserved for young gentlemen who were not as sharp as they ought to be. 'Are you sure this was the house, sir?'

'Yes, of course I am!' Emmett insisted.

'Only, people have been known to mistake one property for another hereabouts. What with the houses all looking the same. What was the name of the person you wished to see?'

Emmett could only look helpless. 'I am sorry, but I don't know. All I can say is that I was invited to a business meeting at this house in apartment number two.'

'A business meeting? How very strange. I have never known anything of that nature taking place here. And if I am not mistaken, the tenant was still in residence on the date you mention. Our tenants are very quiet persons, and do not conduct business at home. I really cannot help you. Good evening.'

The maid was retreating into the hallway and about to close the door when Holmes spoke. 'Perhaps,' he said evenly, 'we might be able to resolve our enquiry if we spoke to the housekeeper. She might recall my friend's visit.'

The maid was now looking at our little assembly as if we were a set of burglars trying to gain admission under false pretences.

'We are content to remain outside if she would be willing to come to the door,' said Holmes. 'What is her name?'

'Mrs Purdue. Wait there. I'll see if she will speak to you.' The maid returned indoors rather rapidly and closed the door.

'This is the house; I am sure of it!' exclaimed Emmett.

'Do you have a written note of the address?' asked Mycroft.

'It was on the invitation. I didn't make a copy, but I remember it, and I recall the stone lions.'

'They are not an uncommon feature in these parts,' said Holmes. 'Was there anything else you can remember about the house you visited apart from the lions and the numbered bells?'

Emmett looked about him helplessly. 'No.' I understood his dilemma. The properties were all of the same design and faced an identical row on the other side of the road. 'But I know the house number. I remember it. I looked at the paper before I pressed the bell. I am sure I am right!'

'Did you come by cab?' asked Mycroft.

'Yes, I took a hansom. I didn't want to be late. But I just gave the driver the name of the street and asked to be set down. I didn't give him the number of the house.'

We were considering the possible usefulness of this evidence when the door opened again, and we were faced with the housekeeper. Mrs Purdue was a tall, rather stout lady of about fifty. I am sure she had a friendly expression but having been briefed by the maid concerning our enquiries she was not employing it.

'Mrs Purdue, I am indebted to you for agreeing to speak to us,' said Holmes, in his most emollient and engaging manner. 'We are hoping to clarify a misunderstanding and would value your observations.' I have seen ladies melt like a warm jelly before Holmes's practised smile, but Mrs Purdue was icily immune.

'Are you the gentleman who claims to have been here before?' she asked, suspiciously. 'Because I have never seen you before in my life.'

'That is I,' said Emmett, coming forward. 'It was the second of last month at five o'clock. I pressed the bell for apartment two and was admitted by a valet, a young man, who conducted me there and opened the door. He had a key. I had been asked to attend a meeting. A business meeting. Unfortunately, the other gentlemen I was to meet were unable to attend and I left after an hour.'

'That apartment is rented by a lady who resides there with her maid,' said Mrs Purdue. 'She does not admit gentlemen callers, and there is no valet in this house. The other two apartments are occupied by retired persons. I wish you good-day, sirs.'

She was retreating inside, and the door was closing, when Emmett darted forward. 'But if you would only let us in and allow us to see the apartment, I am sure I would recall something which would confirm what I say,' he said.

'I will not admit you to this house, and if you do not leave this instant I will send for a policeman,' said the housekeeper.

'If we return with a policeman, might we be allowed to enter?' asked Holmes.

She did not reply and closed the door.

CHAPTER FOURTEEN

Emmett stood trembling on the doorstep, racked with frustration. We calmed him as well as we could and found a nearby hotel with a lounge bar where he was provided with somewhere comfortable to sit and a restorative glass of brandy.

'What am I to do?' he said. 'It was the right house!'

'We must gather our thoughts and first of all consider why anyone would lure you from your desk at that time,' said Holmes. 'Something must have been afoot, something of which we as yet have no knowledge, but knowing what it was would prove useful in our enquiries.'

Mycroft gave a gentle cough. 'Emmett, when you are feeling better you must consider if there is any possibility that you are mistaken, and we have simply gone to the wrong house. Finding the right one could be a great help.'

Emmett said nothing but merely nodded in acknowledgement. I thought that he was still of the opinion that he had not made a mistake but did not have the will to argue.

'Perhaps,' I said, 'you could also try to remember any details of the interior of the house, something which if you went there again and were allowed to look inside, would prove what you have told us of the meeting.'

'I'll try,' he said, miserably, making the brandy vanish almost as fast as his hopes.

'If we have the right street, I fear that any details of the arrangement of rooms and any decorative features created as part of the build would not be helpful,' said Holmes. 'They have all the appearance of a single development. But there may be some distinctive furnishings you might recall. Once we know the house for certain, we may discover the valet, and all will become clear.' He didn't sound hopeful but at least this gave Emmett something to occupy his mind.

For the moment the unhappy clerk appeared more interested in another glass of brandy.

'When you have something to suggest, we can arrange to go there with a police officer who would help us gain admission,' said Holmes.

'Perhaps the lady who lives there rented her apartment out to some gentlemen for business meetings,' I suggested. 'We will find out who they were once she returns. She may not have told the housekeeper what she was doing. The valet might be her brother.'

Emmett was not in a state to respond to encouraging words. We delivered him to his home before he took too much brandy. It is a fine distinction between cheerful and drunk and I think we managed to judge his condition correctly, so he was unlikely to cause his mother unreasonable alarm. He and his widowed mother lived in a three-room apartment in one of the smaller streets off Leicester Square, about twenty minutes' walk from Whitehall. On seeing those humble lodgings, it was brought home to me that if Joshua Emmett and Miss Jessup were ever to marry, the inevitable accumulation of expenses might leave their families in want, if he was unable to advance in his career.

We then retired to Mycroft's club for supper and a discussion. 'Is this a police matter?' I asked. 'If it is, we are duty-bound to report it.'

'Too many things have occurred around the time of Cloudsdale's disappearance,' said Holmes. 'Some may have an innocent explanation; others might be vital clues. There may be many such occurrences involving other men about which we know nothing. The gang might have been making efforts to inveigle some of the officers at Whitehall into their fold. Emmett, because of his circumstances, might have appeared to them to be vulnerable. But I agree with you, Mycroft, he strikes me as a man who would only be tempted into a scheme if it had all the outward appearances of honesty.'

'One thing I will say,' said Mycroft. 'Emmett might not be mistaken about the house, as he did seem very sure about it. Perhaps the housekeeper made it her business to know nothing of what the tenants did. You saw how we were greeted at the door. We will only be able to resolve the issue and learn more if we go back there with a policeman and demand to be admitted. If Emmett has made a mistake he will acknowledge it, but I fear that only a concerted effort by detectives which they are unlikely to make, will identify the right house.'

Holmes nodded. 'Once Emmett has had time for reflection we must return, and I will ask Sergeant Lestrade to accompany us.'

'As ever I will not be of the police party,' said Mycroft, 'but I will let you know as soon as Emmett feels ready. He will be as anxious to resolve this as we are.'

On the following afternoon Holmes, Lestrade and Joshua Emmett arrived at my lodgings in Farringdon. Emmett, who was sober but appeared not to have slept well, if at all, listened without speaking as Holmes described the events of the day before, and what he proposed should now be done.

'So, gentlemen,' said Lestrade, giving Emmett a particularly beady look, 'if I understand you, you wish me to demand entry to a house, a private apartment, where you think — what might have happened?'

'I don't know,' said Emmett, helplessly. 'Only that I was asked to go there for a business meeting of great importance. But no meeting took place.'

Lestrade examined his notebook. 'And you claim that this was on the Tuesday, the day after Cloudsdale was last seen?'

'Yes, it was.'

'You were given no details of the subject of the meeting or who else might attend?'

'No.'

'And when you returned to your desk the next day nothing had been taken, or moved?'

'Not as far as I could see.'

'Do you, in the course of your work, handle documents of a nature which might be valuable if stolen?'

'Not at all.'

Lestrade glanced at Holmes. 'Do you have any observations, Mr Holmes?'

'One possibility is that the event was exactly what it appeared to be, a genuine meeting that was unexpectedly cancelled, although I doubt it,' he said.

'I cannot see why a meeting should have been arranged in a private house,' said Lestrade. 'Is that usual practice?'

'I don't think so,' said Emmett. 'But the circumstances were singular.'

'You mean Cloudsdale?'

'It was the only thing I could think of.'

'Well, you ought to know that enquiries have shown that no other man requested leave at the same time,' said Lestrade.

'But they didn't appear,' protested Emmett.

'I suspect it was a ruse of some sort,' said Holmes. 'I only wish I could examine the invitation. It would be interesting to confirm if the official paper was genuine or a good copy. That might tell us a great deal.'

'And you are sure of the address, Mr Emmett?' queried Lestrade. 'Number twenty-five Cranfield Terrace, you said.'

'Yes. Christmas Day. That is how I remembered it.'

'Did you write it down?'

'No, I didn't need to. I had the invitation with me. I was told to bring it.'

Lestrade drummed his fingers on the table as he considered the conundrum. 'Well, Mr Holmes,' he said at last, 'you have not led me astray before. I will accompany you to the address and see what we can find. But I have no reason to obtain a warrant, and neither can I demand to be admitted. We will see what we will see.'

Emmett thanked him profusely.

'But before we go, I want you to tell me everything you can remember about the interior of the property.'

Emmett nodded. 'I have thought very hard about this. In the hallway was a cupboard for cloaks and hats — the stairs were carpeted, lit by gas. I only saw one room inside the apartment — it was a good size, gas lit, and there was a desk. It was quite a small one, with shallow drawers. Pen, ink, paper, and a blotter were provided. There was seating for a number of people — six to eight, I think. The chairs were arranged in a half circle, so it was obvious they had been set out for a meeting.'

'Any decorative items you can remember? Ornaments? Pictures? Was there a bookshelf?'

'There might have been some ornaments on the mantelpiece, I really didn't pay them any attention. I don't recall any books. There were pictures, yes, the usual portraits of Her Majesty and the Prime Minister, but there was another I especially remember. It was a framed print of a ship. It drew my attention because I wondered if it might have some connection with the meeting. I thought perhaps we were to discuss the design of naval vessels, so I decided to prepare myself by studying it. It was a warship called HMS *Kingston*. I don't believe there was anything unusual about it. I have seen others of its type portrayed before — ironclad, steam-driven, with a single gun turret. When I looked closely, I thought the print itself was not of the best quality. It had a plain wooden frame, and must have been carelessly handled, perhaps it had been dropped, because the frame was cracked in one corner.'

'Which corner?' Holmes demanded.

Emmett considered this, as if trying to recall the image to his mind. 'It was the bottom right corner,' he said at last.

'Perhaps you could draw it for us?' I suggested, fetching paper and a pencil, and placing them in front of him.

'I'm not really an artist,' said Emmett, 'but I'll do my best.' We watched him draw, and something resembling a ship took shape on the paper.

'Is there anything else you can recall?' asked Holmes.

'I'm sorry, no.'

'If something more comes to mind, let us know,' said Lestrade. He rose to his feet. 'Let us go there now, and I hope we can resolve this once and for all.'

We made our way by cab, and soon found ourselves outside the house in question. I could see that Emmett was nervous but cheerfully anticipating being vindicated.

Lestrade approached the door and rang for the housekeeper. The maid appeared, and he showed her his warrant card. 'Sergeant Lestrade of Scotland Yard,' he said, brusquely. 'I would like to speak to Mrs Purdue. May we come in and wait?'

The maid looked at the rest of our party in alarm, but after a moment's consideration, stepped back, and we entered.

'If you could wait here, sir, I will fetch her straight away,' she said, and scurried away.

Emmett looked about him while we waited. 'I am sure I remember that hall cupboard,' he said. 'And the gas lamps, I recall them, too.'

I said nothing but glanced at my companions. I could see that they were thinking the same as I did, that the cupboard and fittings were of a very common type to be found in many houses.

Mrs Purdue appeared, and she looked extremely displeased to be summoned. She looked at the warrant card and this did not improve her mood. 'What is the nature of your enquiry, gentlemen?'

'You will recall the last visit when this gentleman wished to speak to the tenant of apartment two. Has the tenant returned?'

'She has not.'

'Have there been any other visitors asking to be admitted to the apartment?'

'No. All tenants have their own key as well as a key to the front door. Strangers cannot obtain admission on request.'

'What is the name of the tenant of apartment two?'

Mrs Purdue hesitated. 'Miss Noone. And her personal maid.'

'When are they expected back?'

'I don't know, I have yet to hear.'

'What can you tell us about Miss Noone?'

'She is a young lady, well-spoken and respectable.' Mrs Purdue closed her mouth firmly, denoting that this was all she knew or was prepared to say.

'Would you agree to allow us to enter the apartment? Mr Emmett believes he was admitted for a meeting four weeks ago when Miss Noone was absent. Did you give permission for it to be used in that way?'

'I know nothing about it,' said Mrs Purdue firmly. 'I am not sure I believe the gentleman.'

'There is one way to put that to the test,' said Lestrade. 'May we enter and view the property?'

Mrs Purdue's displeasure was now apparent. 'Very well,' she said at last. 'If doing so will settle this ridiculous situation once and for all.'

She turned and led us up the stairs. There was a bunch of keys on a chain at her waist, and she stopped before a door, turned the key and walked in. We followed.

'Oh,' said Emmett as he stood there and looked about him. The room bore no resemblance to the description he had previously given us.

CHAPTER FIFTEEN

Although the fire was not lit and the room therefore quite chilly, it gave the impression of warmth and comfort. There was a woven carpet, in autumnal colours, and draped curtains in a matching hue. The seating consisted of two armchairs and two wooden-backed chairs, all upholstered in striped fabric. The only other furniture was a rectangular table standing against the outer wall beneath the front window. It was laid with a cloth and a cruet set. On the mantelpiece of the marble fireplace were some ornaments and a china vase. Above it was a mirror in a fancy frame. There were a number of pictures on the walls, which appeared to be copies of classical landscapes.

'Are you sure this is where you came for the meeting?' asked Lestrade.

'Yes, yes — I am sure it is. The name of the street, the house number, the apartment number — they are all exactly as I remember, but the room, the furnishings and their arrangement, are quite different.' He looked around frantically, searching for something he could recognise. 'The fireplace — the mouldings are the same.' He glanced up. 'The ceiling rose, and the cornices also.'

'They are the same in all these houses,' said Mrs Purdue, impatiently. 'They are part of a development built at the same time to an identical design.'

Holmes was admiring one of the vases on the mantelpiece. 'May I?' he asked. 'I am interested in porcelain markings.' Mrs Purdue shrugged. Holmes picked up the vase and studied the base. 'Ah yes, as I thought. Made in Staffordshire.' He replaced it.

'Is there anything at all here you remember?' I asked Emmett.

'No, but that table — the shape and size of it. It does look like the desk where I sat, although it wasn't covered with a cloth then. Does it have drawers?' Impulsively Emmett went to the table as if to lift the cloth and peer underneath, but Mrs Purdue strode across his path and stopped him.

'Not one step more!' she said, then turned to Lestrade. 'Sergeant, do you have any reason to believe that a crime has been committed in this house?'

'I — no.'

'Do you have any reason to suspect either Miss Noone or myself, or any occupant of this house of committing a crime?'

'No.'

'I have been extremely generous in allowing you to view the room, but this goes no further. You and your companions have no authority to make any searches here or examine Miss Noone's personal belongings.'

'That is true,' said Lestrade.

'If you have seen everything you need to see then you should leave now.'

'Very well,' said Lestrade. He cast his eyes over our little deputation. 'We should do as Mrs Purdue requests, and leave. I see no reason to return.' Reluctantly, we quitted the apartment, and descended the stairs to the hallway, while Mrs Purdue locked the door. She followed us down, and with a steely eye watched us, to ensure that we actually left the house. 'And Mr Emmett,' Lestrade continued, 'I think you should accompany me to the station as I would like to ask some further questions, about what occurred on the Tuesday when you claim to have come here. I would like to make a record of your statement.'

Emmett sighed. He appeared to have been drained of all energy and spirit. 'Very well. But I have already told the police everything I know.'

'And, just as a precaution, I would like to search your pockets before we go.'

'Why? What are you looking for?'

'It's standard procedure. The only time I ever neglected to make a search, I regretted it, and I have not failed to do so since. Just place everything on the hall table.'

Emmett made no further objection but did as requested. He was not the kind of man who stuffed his pockets to capacity with scraps of paper and pieces of fraying string. The process did not take long and once Lestrade had assured himself that Emmett's pockets were empty he examined what they had produced. I saw a pocketbook, a clip of address cards, a handkerchief, a few coins and a small shiny object, which Lestrade picked up and examined closely.

'What is that?' asked Emmett.

'You tell me, sir,' said Lestrade holding it up for us all to see. Holmes produced his glass and studied it. He said nothing as he returned the glass to his pocket, but his dismay was apparent.

It was a gold cufflink, oval with a beaded edge.

'I have never seen it before,' said Emmett. 'I don't know where it came from.'

'And yet I have seen an identical one very recently,' said Lestrade. 'Joshua Emmett you are under arrest on suspicion of complicity in the murder of Anthony Cloudsdale.' As he continued to deliver the usual caution Emmett's face blanched so rapidly, I thought he was about to faint. He staggered and I seized him by the arm in case he fell.

'I hope you will come quietly, sir?' said Lestrade gently, taking charge of his prisoner's property.

Emmett whimpered and nodded speechlessly.

'Well, here's a fine thing!' exclaimed Mrs Purdue. 'I won't have any of you in my house a moment longer!' We took our leave as quickly and politely as possible.

The cab was still waiting outside, and we boarded it. 'My mother!' cried Emmett. 'She will be beside herself if I am not home soon!'

'I'll send a constable to notify her,' said Lestrade. 'You'll be able to speak to her once I have taken a statement.'

Emmett said not another word for the remainder of our journey, but huddled in a corner of the cab, his initial shock and dismay sliding into a state of profound despair.

I wondered if Holmes and I ought to offer our services for the duty of fetching Mrs Emmett, but of course we were both strangers to her and had no official status. I could not imagine the anguish of a mother, on receiving the dreadful news, and hoped she would be able to see her son and bring him home without too much delay. 'I expect we will know more of what happened in that house when Miss Noone returns,' I said.

'If she ever does,' said Holmes. 'Mrs Purdue may have a nice little trade in short-term tenants who require the hire of private rooms for their own purposes and are willing to rent at a premium. That room might have been cleaned and re-set quite recently.'

Once the cab had deposited Lestrade and Emmett at the police station, Holmes and I proceeded post-haste to Mycroft, who was devastated by the news of his friend's arrest. He admitted that he had been dreading something of the sort, since there had been pressure from senior officials to arrest someone and Emmett's name was the one most frequently mentioned. He was utterly mystified by the finding of the cufflink. 'Can we be sure it is the match to Cloudsdale's or just one that resembles it?' he asked.

'It has the little fault Mrs Cloudsdale mentioned and is of similar age and state of wear,' said Holmes. 'But we must wait for her judgement.'

Mycroft, anxious to have something practical to do, hastened to arrange legal help for his unhappy friend, and went to inform Miss Jessup and her family.

We were hoping to hear that Emmett had been released after questioning, but learned later that Mrs Cloudsdale had confidently identified the cufflink as the match to the one found on the torso, and one of the pair worn by her husband on the day he had disappeared. Emmett was formally charged with being an accessory to murder and would soon be appearing before a bench of magistrates.

CHAPTER SIXTEEN

Holmes, knowing he could rely on Mycroft to do everything possible to support his friend, had decided to pursue another course in the investigation. He determined to find the lair of the gang that had abducted and quite possibly made away with Mr Cloudsdale, in the hope that their arrest would uncover facts that would exonerate Emmett from any knowledge of their crimes.

Unfortunately, London trade directories offered no further clues as to where the secret documents might have been copied, and I had already inspected all the photographic businesses in the areas Cloudsdale might have reached in the time he had available. Holmes regarded this conundrum with some perplexity and decided to place his dilemma before his brother. Their meeting was necessarily brief since Mycroft had managed to secure the services of a leading London solicitor and was about to depart for a consultation.

Holmes's request was only broken by Mycroft's cough for attention. 'Really, Sherlock,' he said tetchily, 'I despair of you sometimes. The answer is quite obvious. The banks of the Thames are a hive of industry and has been for some years. At the same time, businesses have been moving from steam to electricity to power their machinery. You have already eliminated the photographic studios. You need to look instead for another type of business altogether, one that already has a suitable source of power such as an electrical dynamo installed for its trade and might have recently expanded its operations into production of arc lamps, or even experimental photography. There, I leave that with you. We will meet again soon to discuss our findings.' He hurried away.

Holmes had more time available than I did for such exploratory excursions; however, I did not feel able to do other than offer my unqualified assistance. I was not sure how best to approach businesses with our enquiries, as we wanted to avoid alerting the gang to our efforts. If they really had killed and dismembered Mr Cloudsdale, these were dangerous criminals, with no regard for human life, and caution was required.

Our first destination was Stepney. That part of London has a reputation for crimes of every kind throughout its long history, with a population living in the poorest and most overcrowded conditions. I was glad that Holmes's proposed inspection did not require a plunge into some of the more ancient public houses that lined the Limehouse basin, their rickety wooden steps leading in precipitous fashion down to the water, enabling boatmen go directly from their barges for refreshment. Neither did we explore the narrow ill-lit alleys, places where a man might go at night in shameful secrecy for a pipe full of dark oblivion. Holmes, at twenty-three, only observed and absorbed what he saw. I admit that I was horrified years later when I read in Watson's memoirs of Holmes's reckless plunge into that grim and dangerous place during one of his professional enquiries.

I was more comfortable on the broader streets of recent construction, lined with warehouses, workshops and factories. I saw a cement works, and a manufacturer of undersea cables, an advance that had changed the world, only made possible by the waterproof and insulating properties of gutta-percha. There were iron foundries, which manufactured tools and agricultural machinery, and makers of fertiliser, their enormous engines powered by steam. One such company was Premier Iron and Steel Ltd. While principally makers of the standard output of bars, plates, sheets and wire, their sign also mentioned a speciality — the kind of high quality steel required for shipbuilding. Of all the businesses we had seen, this seemed the most likely one to which Cloudsdale had delivered his papers. It would have been unwise for us to make further enquiries in that direction, and I was relieved to see that Holmes — with a brief nod and a firming of his lips — had also come to that conclusion.

His next procedure was to solemnly travel the most likely walking route from that business to the railway station, to identify the place where the attempt had been made on Cloudsdale's life. 'I cannot entirely rule out accident,' said Holmes, 'but while the weather that day was dull, it was not dark; the road is straight, and the traffic not exceptionally dense.' At last, he paused and glanced about. 'There is a side road where a potential assassin might have lurked unseen. A constable is on point not far from the station, but from here, he was just a little too far distant to see what occurred. I think we have the place. Let us see if the constable has anything to enlighten us.' We walked on.

We soon discovered a solid and alert-looking young policeman, close by Stepney railway station, whose main business of the day appeared to be directing travellers.

'Good day,' said Holmes cheerfully. 'I hope you can advise me. I read in the newspapers recently about a dreadful occurrence near this very spot. A man was almost killed after being pushed in front of a moving carriage. My young friend here is of a highly nervous disposition and has been worried about visiting this part of London ever since. I do hope the culprit has been apprehended.'

Holmes always tended when enquiring about such incidents to point me out as the individual who was feeling nervous. I did my best to oblige, but I was sure he could have feigned it himself should he have been so inclined. The policeman, who was scarcely older than myself, smiled at me indulgently. 'It is always wise to take care when crossing the road, sir,' he said. 'No, I am sorry to say that the suspect has not been found. I was asked about it only last week, by a very nervous lady. She told me that she had actually seen the incident happen. The suspect is thought to be a sailor lad, which is not uncommon here, although he was not foreign-looking.'

'A sailor?' asked Holmes, taking out his notebook and pencil and making some jottings. 'How might I recognise him?'

'Well, she only thought he was a sailor as he had pierced ears,' said the policeman.

'I hope he may be found and brought to account before he commits any further crimes,' said Holmes. We thanked the constable and entered the station to take the next train going in a westerly direction, where we were to alight at Fenchurch Street.

'The valet at the Bayswater house had pierced ears,' I said.

'Suggestive but not conclusive,' said Holmes. 'I hope our enquiries will find a connection.'

Fenchurch Street is very different from Stepney. It is a place of business and finance rather than manufacture. There were tall buildings displaying sets of brass plates on their exteriors, with details of the company offices housed within. We found the City Hotel in London Street where Sir Crawford Yates had lunched on the day of Cloudsdale's disappearance. It was an establishment for accommodating and offering the best of food and drink to men who did not have to worry about the price. It was hardly more than a minute's brisk walk from the station.

Holmes inspected the nearby photographer's studio but quickly dismissed it from suspicion. However, as we walked on, we made out an unusual noise. It was a low rumbling sound which became apparent over the general street clamour of carriage wheels and horses' hooves, and we followed it to its source. We were led to a low building with a sign outside bearing the painted legend, 'G. Lambourn and Co., optical lens grinders'.

The main part of the property housed a workshop, which we were able to view through the windows. Inside we saw long tables where men in overalls sat working at lathes. These lathes were not hand-cranked but operated by bands which looped around a set of cogs, one for each lathe. The cogs were made to rotate by a powered device in the centre of the room. The source of the power was not obvious, and we walked about the building, passing by a door, and looking into another window which showed that it led to a kitchen and storeroom, before discovering another door at the back with a notice reading 'No Entry'. The sound which emitted from this door left us in no doubt that a very substantial machine was operating inside.

CHAPTER SEVENTEEN

'How interesting,' said Holmes. He made for the front entrance and pushed open the door. We were faced with a small entrance lobby. Behind a window and occupying the minimum amount of space necessary, there was a tiny office of wooden construction, where a man was seated at a desk. A small opening in the window permitted conversation, and we approached. 'Mr Lambourn?' queried Holmes.

'Yes,' said the man looking up. 'How may I help you?' Lambourn was about fifty, with greying hair, bushy eyebrows, and pince-nez balanced on the bridge of his nose.

'I was wondering,' said Holmes, 'whether in addition to your main business, you also carry out photography.'

'We do not,' said the man. 'But I can direct you to a studio which is nearby.'

'You have no camera and processing equipment here?'

'No, we specialise in lens manufacture, for cameras, spectacles, telescopes, and so on.'

'Ah,' said Holmes. 'And yours is the only business at this premises?'

'It is. Why do you ask?'

I thought Holmes would find some excuse to abandon his questioning at this point and depart, but something about the man's reply, the brief pause between his two utterances, and merest hint of concern in his tone, made him press on. 'Do you by any chance rent out any of your facilities to other businesses?'

I was expecting Lambourn to say he did not, but instead he replied, 'We have done so only once, but it was inconvenient, and I would not do so again.'

'I am sorry to hear that,' said Holmes. 'I hope you did not lose by it.'

'No, far from it. At least not financially. He paid well, and in advance, both for the rent and the use of the electricity from our dynamo machine, but I was not happy with the way it was conducted.' He sighed. 'You are not a friend of Mr MacBrian by any chance? Did he recommend me to you? Is that why you have come here?'

'I have never met a man of that name,' said Holmes. 'Can you describe him?'

'About thirty-five, thin, with dark hair worn long in the way some artists do.'

'And what is his business?'

'More to the point, what is yours?' demanded Lambourn. 'Are you a policeman? Or a debt collector?'

Holmes drew a card from his pocket. 'Neither, but I have advised the police on scientific subjects. My associate pursues the study of surgery.'

'I specialise in ophthalmology,' I said, hoping this would help.

Perhaps it did because Lambourn rose from his desk and came closer to the window, where he scrutinised Holmes's card.

'As to MacBrian's business, I never learned what it was,' said Lambourn. 'He said he was testing a new invention, but refused to say anything about it, as it had not yet been patented. He rented the storeroom at the rear of the building, but demanded exclusive access to it and held all the keys. No-one other than his associates were permitted to enter. He brought in a number of items. I once saw him carrying in what looked like a camera stand but it cannot have been for photography, as he put curtains over the windows, so no-one could see inside.'

'How was the room lit?'

'There is a gas bracket. Quite sufficient for its normal use. After a while I began to wonder if his activities were entirely legal. In fact, I suspected him of being a forger. And he was using my dynamo to power his machinery, which meant that I and my business might have been suspected of involvement. It made me very uncomfortable, and I was considering alerting the police, but then he left, quite suddenly, and I was glad when he did.'

'Did you hear the noise of machinery coming from the room?'

'No, but it might have been overcome by the sound of the dynamo, which can be very loud.'

'When did he rent the room?'

Lambourn returned to his desk and gave us a date from his diary, which Holmes noted. It was one week before Cloudsdale's disappearance. 'He paid a month in advance.'

'You mentioned Mr MacBrian's associates. Who are they?'

'There was only one I saw, an assistant called John. Young fellow. I am not sure I liked the look of him. He didn't seem altogether trustworthy. And there was another man, but I never met him.'

'Did you learn his name?'

'Emmett.'

Even Holmes was unable to disguise his astonishment at hearing this name. 'Emmett?' he exclaimed.

'Yes. Do you know him?'

'I have met a man of that name. But you didn't see him? He did not come here?'

'No. One morning MacBrian said to his assistant, "John, remember you are to see Mr Emmett this afternoon." And John said, "Why am I to see Emmett?" And MacBrian said, "On a matter of great importance" or some such words. Then they saw I had overheard them and walked away. And the very next morning they had gone. Without any warning. I inspected the room, but they had removed all their property.'

'What strange behaviour,' said Holmes. 'I wonder if the Emmett who they saw was the man I have met, or his relation. What day did this occur?'

Lambourn consulted his desk diary again. 'Here it is — MacBrian and his associate have gone.' The date he gave us was the Wednesday after Cloudsdale disappeared. It did not elude us that the proposed meeting MacBrian had mentioned was on the same afternoon that Emmett said he had been called to the Bayswater apartment.

'Perhaps if you see Mr Emmett, you might ask him who Mr MacBrian is and what is his business,' said Lambourn. 'If it is perfectly innocent then that would put my mind at rest.'

'I shall certainly do so,' said Holmes. 'I do have one question which might assist me. Was there anything at all unusual about Mr MacBrian's assistant? His clothing, any distinctive marks, or scars?'

'I did notice he had pierced ears,' said Lambourn. 'Is that the fashion amongst young men nowadays? It is very peculiar.'

'And you inspected the room immediately after they vacated it?'

'Yes.'

'Was there any residue or rubbish, or spillage which suggested what they had been doing?'

'No, nothing at all.'

'No unusual odours?'

'There was a slight smell of — I can hardly describe it — a kind of burning. But what they might have been burning I couldn't say.'

'Any chemical odours? Acrid? Sharp?'

'I thought I detected an acidic odour, although there were no chemicals in the room. And something unpleasant, almost like bad eggs. I had to open the windows to air the room.'

'It might assist me to answer your concerns if I examined the room.'

'I don't see why not.'

Lambourn left his office and called one of the men from his table in the workroom, asking him to sit at the desk in case of visitors, while we were shown the room.

The storeroom, which he unlocked from the exterior, was a plain square with flagstone flooring and whitewashed walls. Some simple shelving held machine parts, and wooden boxes of the business's products. Holmes proceeded to study the whole of the space in detail with his glass.

'There is a hole bored through the wall, where the wire connecting his machinery with the dynamo entered the room,' said Lambourn. 'Oh, and we had to move the shelving and their contents to our workroom while he was here. He didn't want any of our employees coming in and witnessing what he was doing.'

'He had the key to the exterior door?'

'Yes.'

'So if he had had visitors, he could have admitted them without your knowing?'

'Yes.'

'Whatever machinery he was employing it must have given off a great deal of heat,' said Holmes. 'It has left a scorch mark on the wall. There has been an attempt to cover it with whitewash, not entirely successful as I think it was done in a hurry, but visible if one looks closely.'

Once Holmes's examination was complete, he requested and received Mr Lambourn's business card.

'You will let me know if you discover anything more about this man and his business?' asked Lambourn.

'If he is innocent I will advise you,' said Holmes. 'If he is a criminal, you may be required to identify him.'

'I have been making a study of the processes involved in photography,' said Holmes as we departed. 'There are several critical stages starting well before the plate is placed in the camera and exposed to the light and continuing afterwards in order to achieve a good result.

'I think that there can be no doubt that Mr Lambourn's storeroom was used as a photography studio to take pictures under the light of an arc lamp, when most people would have thought that impossible,' he continued. 'They hired the room, brought in the equipment, tested it, and waited for Cloudsdale to be directed there. One thing they may not have anticipated is the amount of heat given off by their lamp, the result of which they were obliged to conceal.

'When Cloudsdale arrived, speed was essential in order to convince him that the papers were not being opened and photographed. One of the men was no amateur in that respect. He knew how to use the equipment, and also how to employ chemicals to develop and fix the image on the glass plate. He must have worked in that line of business. Perhaps he still does.

'The next step, which does require the light of the sun, and more time, is creating the photograph from the plate. If our man carries out this duty in his employment or has his own business, he will be able to include the plates he has taken, without it being noticed or the secret contents revealed. The weather reports show that in the days after the men left their makeshift studio there was clearer weather, and he would have been able to produce images from the plates.'

'If they hired the room for a month, they might have carried that out there,' I said.

'Possibly, yes, there is a flat roof space they might have used. The trouble and expense they went to in establishing that studio suggests to me that their intention was to make use of it for some time. But I think after Cloudsdale became suspicious they decided to go in case enquiries about him led to them.'

'What do you think happened to him?'

'If he is dead, he might have been waylaid, abducted, held somewhere, interrogated, and ultimately killed. If by some chance he is alive, he may be in fear, and hiding. But I agree with Mycroft, the man is dead. Mrs Cloudsdale has received no note from her husband and made no unusual visits. She accepts that she is a widow.'

'So Cloudsdale might have been killed on the day he disappeared, or if he was interrogated first, a day or so afterwards? It could even have been on the day that Emmett went to that meeting?'

'That is certainly possible. But I do now have a new line to pursue. The camera and other photographic materials are not hard to come by. The lamp, on the other hand, is another matter. They may have had to arrange for one to be made. I will explore that possibility and see if it leads us anywhere.'

CHAPTER EIGHTEEN

The following afternoon Holmes and I were invited to the offices of Ineson and Randall, solicitors, for a meeting. A tired-looking Mycroft met us outside. He had been spending much of his time and energy supporting Miss Jessup and her family, and Mrs Emmett, all of whom had been plunged into misery and bewilderment by recent events. The conversations he had shared with them had taken the form of repeatedly turning the facts over and over but arriving at no useful conclusions.

The location, size and inner furnishings of the solicitors' offices told us that this was an old established firm of reputation, and we were about to see one of the senior partners. I wondered briefly who would be paying for this consultation but decided not to ask. It could only be Mycroft Holmes, generously supporting his old friend. We were greeted and conducted to Mr Ineson's office by a young man, who from the dignity of his deportment and the quality of his attire I thought must be at the very least a junior partner, but who, I later learned, was secretary to Mr Ineson, the solicitor who would be acting for Emmett.

Mr Ineson, a spare, grey-haired gentleman sat like a benevolent noble in his personal domain, enveloped in the fragrance of antique wood, old leather, and new polish. We assembled before him to be granted audience.

'I have had a lengthy consultation with Mr Emmett, and also spoken to the police who are looking into his case,' said Ineson. 'There is no doubt that several serious crimes have been committed, but there is no firm evidence of the location of any of those in which they believe Mr Emmett may have been involved. Neither have the police been able to identify or apprehend the other persons implicated. The proceedings have been passed to Westminster Police Court in Vincent Square, where Mr Emmett has at least the advantage of the new cells there which are a great improvement in comfort and cleanliness to what went before.'

'I was permitted a brief visit,' said Mycroft. 'The poor fellow is distraught. He can hardly appreciate that what has happened is actual rather than a bad dream from which he will soon awaken. He denies all involvement with the disappearance of Mr Cloudsdale. He knows nothing of a criminal trade in documents. He cannot explain any of the circumstances that have drawn attention to him, except that they must be a coincidence, or he has been mistaken for another man.'

'It is a great pity,' said Ineson, 'that Mr Emmett has been unable to provide any information which might prove useful to his defence. I have spoken to his mother, and Miss Jessup, both of whom are adamant that my client is an honest, hardworking man, greatly liked by all, with not an enemy in the world. They find it impossible that he should do a dishonourable or blameworthy act.' He puffed a little exhalation of regret. 'Of course, there are men who hide foul natures under such a convincing mask of concealment that they earn the trust of all those who know them. When they are exposed, it is always a terrible shock to everyone, and their families often refuse to believe the clearest and most damning evidence. I am not saying that Mr Emmett is such a man, only that in his defence I would like to be able to offer something more than the protestations of his mother, his fiancée, and an old friend. Character witnesses have their place but will carry little weight if unsupported by facts. They are not evidence.'

'I have new information which I acquired yesterday and which I have already passed to the police,' said Holmes. 'I have made a note for you of my findings.' He passed a written paper to Mr Ineson. 'They do not, unfortunately, assist your client. We have located the place to where we believe Mr Cloudsdale was lured on his way to deliver the papers, and where the contents were quickly copied using a recent experimental process in photography. It was a room hired from a company, Lambourn and Co., optical lens grinders in the vicinity of Fenchurch Street. Mr Cloudsdale may not have realised what was happening, and I think he may have been led to believe that the procedure had official approval. I do not think Mr Lambourn was involved; in fact, he was suspicious of the activities being carried out on his premises and was about to report them to the police when the hirers vacated the room without warning. I also think I have found the place where Cloudsdale was assaulted after delivering the papers in Stepney, and there is a witness who will show that the young man who carried out this assault fits the description of the man who played the part of the valet at the meeting to which Emmett was called, and also assisted at the copying of the papers. He was heard to be addressed as "John". There was a policeman on duty at Stepney station who interviewed this witness and I have passed his collar number to Scotland Yard.'

Mr Ineson looked impressed, as he had every reason to be, and made a careful study of Holmes's report, nodding his approval as he read.

'The man who appeared to be in charge of the photography was called MacBrian,' Holmes continued. 'That may not be his real name, of course. I was told he was about thirty-five, thin, and wears his hair long. On the morning of the day after Mr Cloudsdale's disappearance, he mentioned to his assistant that they had a meeting that afternoon with a man called Emmett. Has your client mentioned an acquaintance of that name and description?'

'He has not, but I will pose the question,' said Ineson. 'That comment would have been made on the same day as that on which my client was later called to this secret meeting he has described. I have made enquiries, but no-one seems to know anything about it.'

'Has Miss Noone returned from her travels?' asked Holmes, his tone implying that he was highly sceptical that such an event had occurred, or ever would.

'Not yet, but I hope to be informed when she does,' said Ineson, whose glance suggested that he shared Holmes's point of view.

Mycroft grunted. 'I believe the Bayswater constables have been asked to look out for her return, and their efforts are being supplemented by the keen eyes of delivery boys in that area, who will report to me.'

'The housekeeper, Mrs Purdue, has been singularly unhelpful,' said Ineson, 'but there are no legal powers to search the apartment.' He sighed. 'I will do my best for Mr Emmett. It is unfortunate that all he can tell me is that he is innocent of any wrongdoing.'

'I can only assume that he has somehow become unwittingly entangled in the machinations of some clever criminals who are able to cover their own tracks, leaving him exposed,' said Mycroft. 'He may have carried out actions which he has not appreciated were part of their plans and have given him the appearance of guilt. Do you know what charges will be brought, and what evidence the police will produce?'

'They are not at present revealing their hand,' said Ineson, 'but I would think there will be charges of conspiracy to steal government papers, or even, dare I say it, commit murder or treason. If we can persuade the magistrates that he was simply an innocent dupe, we may see the charges dropped, but what may happen to his future career, we cannot know. Evidence? He knew Cloudsdale, he knew of his work as a trusted courier. He was seen with the same woman Cloudsdale met with, the woman with the yellow flowers in her hat, who has not yet been identified. He has no credible alibi for a certain afternoon which is believed to be the one where the meeting took place mentioned by MacBrian. This man we now know must have been instrumental in copying the documents, and his associate may have been the same man who attempted to murder Cloudsdale. My client has received money, a fifty-pound note for which he is unable or unwilling to account. His only explanation as to its origins has been proven false. And lastly, and worst of all, a cufflink known to have belonged to Mr Cloudsdale, one of a pair of which the other was found with the torso identified as that of the missing and now presumably murdered man, was found in Mr Emmett's pocket. I have seen men hanged for far less evidence than that.'

'I rather fear,' said Holmes to Mycroft, 'that your friend has been drawn into a spider's web. Perhaps he is unable or too afraid to extricate himself.'

'Afraid, yes,' said Mycroft. After a brief interlude of contemplation, he continued. 'Let us suppose that he has, in all innocence, been associating with persons he was led to believe were engaged on official business. He might have been told there were issues of national importance and sworn to secrecy. He has only now come to realise that he was being misled. He can exonerate himself by giving evidence against these persons, but following Cloudsdale's disappearance he must fear that by doing so he will sign his own death warrant. They might have some other hold over him, too, threats to his mother, and Miss Jessup. He would condemn himself rather than have any harm come to them.' Mycroft took a handkerchief from his pocket and pressed it to his forehead, then his eyes. We allowed him a few moments to recover himself.

'But he has let slip the one detail which suggests there is some connection,' said Ineson. 'The valet with the pierced ears. If it can be shown that the valet was also MacBrian's assistant and Cloudsdale's assailant, then a prosecution will say that this establishes proof of my client's involvement.'

There was a long silence while we digested these thoughts.

'Gentlemen,' said Ineson. 'I suggest that you take no further action until my client has appeared in the police court. We should then know a great deal more about his future. The police have been working to uncover fresh evidence and identify witnesses. I, too have been making enquiries, and your contributions will be extremely valuable.'

We thanked him and waited to be called before Emmett's forthcoming appearance before the magistrates.

CHAPTER NINETEEN

The hearing at the Westminster Police Court commenced promptly at 10 o'clock two days later. This substantial building comprised not only the courtroom and cells, and premises for the use of magistrates and their officers, but the Metropolitan Police of B division, with accommodation for some of the men. The courtroom itself was built for practicality, devoid of unnecessary decoration but generous in size, with plenty of space for both officials and the public.

While taking our places we looked around us to gather who might be in attendance and what their interest in the case might be.

The earliest arrivals were three ladies who sat side by side. They were heavily veiled, and clasped hands in mutual support. I felt sure I recognised the trim figure of Miss Jessup and guessed that the other two were Mrs Jessup and Mrs Emmett. Mrs Cloudsdale arrived next, dressed in widow's weeds, together with her son, Gregory, also now in mourning.

I was not greatly surprised to see Mrs Collett, who announced herself by her odour long before she came into view. She placed herself firmly on the front row, where she sat with a sour look, ready to take issue with anything that prompted her disagreement. Mrs Purdue was not there, but her maid was. I thought she must have been directed to attend and report back to her mistress.

It was troubling to see a substantial array of witnesses, all of whom, I feared, would have material to bolster the prosecution's case. There were two men I did not recognise. A stout individual of about forty years of age, wearing an oily-looking wig, and a broad-shouldered man in his fifties, with a large white moustache, whose gait suggested arthritic knee joints. The younger, Mycroft advised us, was the manager of the tea shop where Cloudsdale had been seen in the company of the lady with the yellow flowers in her hat, and the other was Mr Drummond, hall porter at the Whitehall offices.

There was the usual cluster of eager reporters and the curious public. The case had already aroused significant interest and I felt sure that if it ever came to trial, it would be a newspaper sensation, discussed in every club and hostelry, and across every tea table in the land. Shortly before the proceedings were due to open, another veiled lady entered alone, and sat quietly at the back of the courtroom.

Mr Ineson was seated at a table reserved for the legal men, together with the counsel. Mycroft, who had kept himself well-informed, pointed out the notable figures and their various functions. The magistrates were led by Mr Edmund Woolrych, a gentleman in his sixties respected for his acumen, who had sat on the Westminster bench for many years. This was not a trial as such, the bench would not make a judgement as to guilt. Rather the hearing was to determine whether there was a case to answer on the charges, and if so, the prisoner would then be committed for trial at a higher court.

The prosecution solicitor was a youthful-looking Mr Reader. A more senior gentleman was a barrister, Mr Besley, who would be acting for the defence if there was to be a subsequent trial.

An officer of the court called for silence, and Joshua Emmett was brought up from the cells. I could see that he had made every effort with his appearance in order to look as presentable as possible, but there was no mistaking the strain upon his features, and the repeated clasping of his fists at his sides showed the strength of his resolve to maintain his courage and dignity. He glanced at the three ladies, and I could see that he knew who they were and was comforted by their presence.

The proceedings opened with a reading of the charges made against Joshua Emmett; conspiracy to commit treason by allowing a foreign power sight of secret government papers, conspiracy to abduct Mr Anthony Cloudsdale, and accessory to the unlawful killing of Mr Anthony Cloudsdale. Although there were no words spoken in the assembly, there was the sound of intakes of breath, and little gasps in places. The ladies who sat together gripped each other's hands more tightly.

We attended closely to the evidence as this was an indication of what would be presented if the prisoner came to trial. Holmes had once told me that the best evidence given in any case was always the freshest, the immediate impressions. These were the first witness statements, if one could get them, otherwise that given at inquests and police courts. The trial might follow months later, and memories could change significantly over time, not necessarily for the better.

Mr Reader rose and presented an outline of the events which had brought the prisoner to his current situation; the disappearance of Mr Cloudsdale, after delivering the papers, the finding and identification of the torso. He said that the witnesses to be brought before the court would show that the prisoner had been seen with a lady who had also had a clandestine meeting with Mr Cloudsdale. The prisoner was known by name to a Mr MacBrian, the man believed to have received the documents carried by Cloudsdale and copied them. The prisoner had on his own admission met MacBrian's associate, who was also believed to be the person who conducted a murderous assault on Mr Cloudsdale. Emmett's alibi for the evening following Cloudsdale's disappearance was a meeting connected with his work, a claim which was unsupported by any witness, and demonstrably untrue. The next day, the prisoner received an envelope containing the sum of fifty pounds and provided an explanation for this receipt which could not be sustained. When arrested, a cufflink belonging to Mr Cloudsdale which he had worn on the day of his disappearance, had been found in the prisoner's pocket.

It was a grim catalogue, and I believe we were very unpleasantly aware that much of the evidence being presented by the prosecution had been uncovered by our efforts. Holmes, who refused to allow any trace of emotion to affect his judgement, had a face of stone, while Mycroft, who was of a softer hearted disposition, was very much moved.

There were witnesses as to the character and trustworthiness of Mr Cloudsdale. Mr Drummond, a stalwart of the porter's desk at Whitehall for many years, was able from his meticulously kept records to testify as to the exact time Mr Cloudsdale had departed on his mission, adding that there was no record of his return. It was suggested to him that he might have occasionally been absent from his post during the day, an implication at which he was deeply offended. He said he had a reliable deputy, a Mr Osmond, and this meant that there was always a man on duty during the hours when the office was open. The desk was never left unattended.

Mr Lambourn told the court of MacBrian's rental of a portion of his business premises, and the mention of Emmett by name.

The manager of the tea shop whose name was Mr Bradley, testified that a week before Mr Cloudsdale's disappearance he had seen the deceased taking tea with a young lady who wore a hat trimmed with a spray of yellow silk flowers. A few days afterwards, he had seen this young lady again, wearing the same hat, but this time she had been walking in the park in conversation with the prisoner. At this statement, Emmett gasped. He turned to Mr Ineson and shook his head in a very determined fashion.

Young Joe the telegraph boy told of the lady who had given him a shilling and a flower to deliver the envelope to the prisoner. He still had the flower in his pocket, a little flattened, but still noticeably yellow, and showed it to the court.

I noticed that Miss Jessup had not been asked to describe the chance encounter in the street with the lady with the yellow flowers in her hat. This might have been due to her state of distress, and I could only hope that the prosecution counsel would not require her to testify should there be a trial.

Surgeon Bond described his examination of the torso and the identification of the shirt and discovery of the cufflink belonging to Cloudsdale. Sergeant Lestrade next gave evidence. He had investigated the prisoner's claim that he had been lured to an apartment for an important meeting connected with his employment on the day after Mr Cloudsdale's disappearance. He had visited this apartment and spoken to the housekeeper, but there was no evidence that any such meeting had taken place there. On deciding to take the prisoner to the police station to obtain a formal statement, the usual searches had discovered a cufflink in Emmett's pocket which matched the one found with the torso. This had been shown to Mrs Cloudsdale who identified it as her husband's.

The last witness was Chief Inspector Thomas Foinette of B division, the officer who had interviewed Emmett and taken his statement. This statement was read out in full and consisted of Emmett's denial of any involvement in what had been done with the papers, and the fate of Mr Cloudsdale. He insisted that his original account of the meeting in Bayswater had been wholly truthful, and he had never met anyone of the name and description of Mr MacBrian.

Mr Besley then rose to address the court. 'I will be reserving my defence at this point since enquiries are still under way. There are numerous witnesses who have known the accused for many years, and who will testify that the crimes with which he has been charged are of a nature quite foreign to his character. I anticipate being able to show that the evidence of the prosecution is a tissue of mistaken identity and coincidence. I therefore ask for an adjournment of the proceedings for another two weeks, on which date I shall show that there is no case to answer and request the release of the prisoner.' He sat down, but his meaning was very clear. He had no evidence to help his client and wanted time to find some.

After some consultation, the board of magistrates came to a decision to commit Emmett for trial on all the charges at the Central Criminal Court. I thought Emmett would collapse. He seemed to shrink in size, and his face fell as the pent-up determination to keep his calm and dignity left him. Then he glanced at Miss Jessup, took a deep breath, and stood firm once more. The constables took him down to the cells.

Mrs Collett pushed herself violently from her chair and favoured the magistrates with a glare of disapproval. I almost expected her to make an outburst, but instead she stamped away, seething with annoyance. I suppose she might have been called by the defence to oppose the decision of the inquest, but I did not think she would have made an impressive witness.

The veiled lady who sat alone quickly rose to her feet and turned to leave, but Holmes, who had been keeping an eye on her, swiftly followed. 'Excuse me, Miss,' he said, holding out a folded pocket handkerchief. 'I think you may have dropped this.'

She appeared momentarily startled at his approach. 'You are mistaken, sir; that is not mine,' then she hurried away. Holmes tucked the handkerchief into his pocket, and followed her as unobtrusively as possible, but re-joined us a minute or two later. 'As I surmised, she is here to watch the proceedings. She has darted aboard a passing hansom and eluded us. But I think I have heard her voice before.'

'I am afraid,' said Ineson, 'that given the weight of suspicion and my client's failure to account for the evidence, that result was inevitable. Our main hope is that we do have time, at least a month or two before the trial is likely to take place, in which we may be able to mount a convincing defence. I remain of the belief that Emmett knows a great deal more than he is saying, but is afraid to do anything other than deny the accusations. I intend to bring his mother and fiancée to see him and plead with him to tell the truth in the hope that he will relent and tell all. If he has been drawn into something against his better judgement and played only a minor role, perhaps under threat, he may escape with a light sentence. That is my current way of thinking. I must have the means to rebut the testimony brought against him, but he has given me nothing.'

'If you can obtain permission for me to see him, I would be very grateful,' said Mycroft. 'Perhaps I can appeal to our old friendship. I will do all I can to assist him.'

Ineson promised to do so, and we left the court, still clinging onto the slowly vanishing threads of hope.

CHAPTER TWENTY

We were not of course present at the painful visit paid by Mrs Emmett and Miss Jessup to Joshua Emmett in his cell at Newgate, where he was being held on remand. Mycroft also went, but separately, to see his old friend, and when we met with him again, he looked pale and tired. 'I must assume that there is some hold over him which cannot be loosened,' he said, despairingly. 'He denies everything. He says he cannot reveal his associates because he has none, and neither is he able to explain the evidence which appears so strong against him. My only conclusion is that the villains have threatened his family and Miss Jessup and he is willing to sacrifice his freedom, even his life, in order to keep them safe. What a noble fellow he is! If you are correct, Holmes, and the woman who was observing the committal has reported to her masters, they will now know that he has resolutely kept his silence. If there is any help for him it must come from us.'

'Will the statement he gave to the police be presented at the trial?' I asked.

'Most probably,' said Mycroft. 'It will not help him.'

'Judging by what we have learned about MacBrian and his associate, I fear that even if they are apprehended, they are unlikely to give evidence in his favour,' said Holmes. 'Rather the reverse.'

'Criminals of that type do not hesitate to pile blame on others for their misdeeds,' said Mycroft. He sighed. 'Emmett's own mother has failed to move him. I was told that the poor lady actually fell to her knees before him, and begged him to tell the truth, but all he would say was that he had already told all he knew and could say no more.'

'And Miss Jessup?'

Mycroft shook his head. 'She stood by and listened, and wept, but that was all. I asked him if there was anything I might do to help him, but he only said that I should watch over Miss Jessup and be as a loving brother to her. Of course I will do so.'

'Would Mrs Emmett and Miss Jessup permit me to pay them a visit?' asked Holmes. 'It may be that there is some small incident they have observed, something apparently trivial, which could furnish a clue as to the true state of affairs.'

Mycroft nodded. 'I will ask them. I am sure they will agree.'

'And I think it might be best if only I and Stamford were to speak to them on this occasion,' Holmes added. 'I can see, Mycroft, that you are deeply affected by your friend's plight, and what this case needs is a calm and clear-headed appreciation and examination of the facts.' Mycroft frowned but did not disagree. 'Continue any other work you may be undertaking for the time being,' said Holmes, 'but allow me this.'

The home of Joshua Emmett and his mother was tidily kept and shared with an elderly aunt who acted as a general maid and cook. Mrs Emmett was a lady of about sixty, and I saw in her the same determination as her son to bear up under an almost intolerable strain. Miss Jessup was keeping her company, and they thanked us profusely for our efforts to assist the prisoner. In the face of the obvious question not being asked, Holmes reassured them that although he had some experience in solving mysteries, he was not a professional detective and expected no reward for his work.

This statement was met with some relief.

The aunt brought in a tray of tea things, which included bread and butter and some rather dry plain cake. 'I am very sorry, this is all we have,' said Mrs Emmett apologetically.

'Oh, but this is perfectly good, in fact it is better for the digestion,' said Holmes, kindly.

'It is,' I agreed, with as much enthusiasm as I could muster.

The tea was poured, and plates distributed, then the aunt left us to our conference. 'I would like, if you are amenable, to ask some simple questions, in order that I might learn as much as I can about the circumstances of this unusual case,' said Holmes.

'I will answer your questions whatever they may be,' said Mrs Emmett.

'To begin with, can you let me know how your son appeared to you in the weeks before Mr Cloudsdale vanished? Was he his usual self or was he troubled by anything?'

'He was quite his usual self,' said Mrs Emmett. 'In fact, he was happy about his recent betrothal, and he and Millicent were constantly talking of the wedding and the life they would have together. Of course, they knew it would be a long engagement, but that is the way of these things.'

'Joshua was hoping for a promotion, and a larger salary so he could put aside more savings,' said Miss Jessup. 'And I am already making my wedding gown, which will be very fine indeed.' Her lips trembled as she said this, since the promotion and wedding both appeared even further away than before. 'But we will marry,' she said, determinedly, 'we will, even if we have to live on almost nothing.'

'How well did he know Mr Cloudsdale?' asked Holmes.

'Joshua rarely spoke about his work,' said the anxious mother. 'I am not sure I ever heard him say the name before he mentioned that a man had left the office and not returned.'

'What were his usual hours?'

'Nine in the morning to five in the afternoon. But he did sometimes stay later if there was work to be finished. He promised to do his best to be home by six o'clock at the latest, but said he would send a message if he was ever to be later than that.'

'The day after Mr Cloudsdale disappeared — it was a Tuesday — did he send you a message?'

'Yes, he said he had been called to a meeting and would be home later than usual. He arrived at about a quarter to seven.'

'What did he tell you about the meeting?'

'Nothing. It would have been unusual if he had. He only said that he had been told there would be another, but he had not yet been advised of the date.'

'How did he seem when he returned?'

'It was a long day, and he was tired and hungry. That was all.'

'Do you recall the day after, when the envelope arrived?'

'I do indeed.'

'Can you describe what happened?'

'Yes, he came to me and said, "Here's a strange thing just been delivered" and showed me the envelope. I looked at it, but I didn't recognise the writing. When he opened it he found a banknote inside. Fifty pounds.'

'What did he say?'

'He was astonished. We both were. He looked inside to see if there was a note with it, but there was nothing. "I wonder who could have sent me this?" he said.'

'When I spoke to him, he suggested it might have come from his cousin, Charles Guthrie, to whom he had lent some money,' said Holmes. 'A repayment of the loan with interest.'

'No, Charles died in prison without a penny to his name,' said Mrs Emmett. 'He had some funds when he was put on trial, but it was all forfeit as it came from his crimes.'

'And your son did not know his cousin was dead?'

'He did not even know his cousin was in prison,' she said. 'I never told him. I thought it best. I hoped no-one would hear of our shame. What if his employers had learned of it? How would that have affected his work, his future, if it was known he had a criminal in the family? Charles was my poor late sister's son. The man she married was a bad lot and he took after his father.'

'Can you suggest who might have sent that money?' asked Holmes.

Neither lady had any suggestions to offer.

'Has there been anything unusual in his behaviour or his mood in the last few weeks?' asked Holmes. 'The most trivial circumstances could be of value.'

'Nothing at all,' said Mrs Emmett, and Miss Jessup agreed.

'It may be,' said Holmes, carefully, 'that there is something preventing him from telling what he knows. I don't mean anything of a criminal nature. I urge you to consider what that might be. Some danger, which is worse than what he now faces. I know you will exert all your influence on him and ask him to speak out and save himself.'

It had not escaped my notice that Miss Jessup had said very little during our interview, but at Holmes's appeal, she put down her teacup so abruptly, so angrily, that I was startled by the noise.

'But what could he say?' she demanded. 'He has already told all that he can. The accusations may look bad, but I truly believe that there is nothing in them, and Joshua is innocent of all wrongdoing. I know him, and I cannot, I *will* not believe he is guilty of anything. It is not in his character. He cannot speak out as you suggest he should as he knows nothing. All I can do is comfort him.'

The depth of her emotion, her utter unshakeable belief in her fiancé, made a powerful impression on me.

We were to learn no more that day. Before we took our leave Holmes entreated both ladies to promise to search their memories in the hope of discovering anything which might prove to be vital for the defence of Joshua Emmett.

CHAPTER TWENTY-ONE

Next morning I was undertaking a dissection in the anatomy room, a rather delicate one, exploring the muscles which controlled the movement of the eyes, when I heard some unusually strident voices in the corridor, one of which sounded uncomfortably familiar. The distraction obliged me to pause in my work. The door opened and a porter looked in. His expression, which bordered on panic, confirmed my fears.

'Mr Stamford? There is a person here asking — well, demanding to see Mr Holmes. I told her to wait in the visitors' room, but she won't. You don't happen to know where Mr Holmes is, do you?' he added plaintively.

At that moment, he staggered aside as Mrs Collett pushed past him. She strode into the room and looked rapidly about her, as if she expected to see Holmes attempting to hide behind a bench and was prepared to drag him out from concealment. 'He's not in here!' she announced. Then she fastened her eyes on me and snarled, 'I know you! You were at the mortuary and the inquest and the police court with Mr Holmes! I never heard more rubbish spoken in all my life!'

'I was,' I said, washing my hands and tidying my bench, since I could see it was pointless to do any further work until Mrs Collett had found Holmes, neither was it advisable to let her continue her exploration of the college unsupervised. 'Allow me to help you. He may be working in the library, but if I take you there, you must promise me not to go in, as only students are permitted.' The image of a battalion of burly orderlies attempting to eject Mrs Collett flashed before my eyes and it was not an attractive sight. 'I will go in and see if he is available.'

'Well, as long as I can speak to him,' she said.

I reassured the porter that I would be able to progress matters from there and he disappeared with noticeable relief. 'What business do you have with him?' I asked, as we made our way to the library.

'It's about my husband, Dickie,' she said. 'I went to the police again, and told them, either you prove that that thing that was pulled out of the river is what's left of him, and go and find the rest, so I can get him buried proper, or, if you think it isn't him, then he is still missing, and you should be out looking for him. That Mrs Cloudsdale, she wants to bury it as well, but she won't until she has a whole body. But I know it's him. They've still got him in pickle.'

'What did the police say?'

'All I know is, they are going by the inquest, that it was this Mr Cloudsdale, and they still haven't found any more of him. And they say they are keeping a lookout for my husband, but no other bodies have been found that could be him. There was only one sergeant who was any help at all, Lestrade. He said that the only man he knew who could find the answer was Mr Holmes. "Is he a detective?" I said. "Well, a sort of one," he said. "But he is very good. And he don't charge anything; he just likes to find answers." And he said I would find him here. So I thought, that sounds like what I have to have.'

'Holmes does like to solve mysteries,' I confirmed as we reached the door of the library. 'But here we are. Now, I have to creep in and be very quiet as I am not allowed to speak where people are at their studies, but I can find out if he is here, so please wait outside. I won't be long.'

'Funny place, this,' she said. 'I'll wait, but you be quick.'

As it so happened, Holmes was immersed in a volume of anatomical sketches, but when I alerted him, he understood that something was afoot, and we were able to converse at the librarian's desk. 'Mrs Collett is here, she wants to see you,' I whispered. He did not look delighted by this news, but simply gave a curt nod, handed back his books, and followed me into the corridor, where our visitor was waiting.

'Mrs Collett,' he said politely. 'Kindly accompany us to the visitors' room and we will speak there.'

When we arrived, there were two visitors already in the room, but on Mrs Collett entering and thumping her broad frame onto a seat, bringing her particular odour to the atmosphere, they decided to go and stand outside in the corridor. Mrs Collett repeated what she had told me and expressed her extreme displeasure at the lack of any progress, using language I had never expected to hear from the lips of a female. We established that her husband worked as a warehouseman for a man called Roberts in Bermondsey Wall by the wharf side. They lived in nearby Tooley Street, above a tripe shop, where she worked as a tripe dresser. She had been expecting him home after his working day was done — it was the Friday, four days after Mr Cloudsdale had last been seen — allowing for his usual stops for refreshment on the way. For a relatively short street, Bermondsey Wall provided a wide choice of hostelries, which she named as The Fleece, The Grapes, The Mariners, The Admiral, and The Justice. He had not returned, and she had had no news of him since.

Holmes listened patiently and established that Collett might have visited any or even all of the hostelries on the night in question. 'You have said that he might have fallen into the river,' he said.

'Well, that was what I thought at first, before that body turned up,' Mrs Collett said. 'But not now I don't. I mean, how did it get under the bridge on the other side? Things float up and down the river, not across it. It didn't walk across, did it? Anyhow, what with his bad foot he never walked far. Someone put it there. Someone killed him and cut him up. The rest of him might still be down there, all tangled up in some rubbish.'

'You are still quite sure the torso is that of your husband?'

'I think so. You'd only have to find an arm or a leg to prove it. But if it isn't his, he might still be dead and there is a whole body to find.'

'Then I shall help you find him,' said Holmes. 'I will start in Bermondsey and see if there were any sightings of him that night, and if so, where.'

'The police haven't found nothing.'

'The police are a fine resource, but they are not Sherlock Holmes,' said my friend.

'Take my advice, don't go dressed too fancy,' she said. 'They steal clothes down there. There's a rag merchants next to the horse slaughterer in Tooley Street. He'd have those off your back.'

'Thank you for that warning. I can't promise success, but I will do what I can. It may take some time.'

'And you don't want money?' she asked. 'Because I don't have much, not now, without Dickie's wages coming in, just what I get for scraping the tripe. I could get some boiled tripe for you if you want, Mr Holmes?'

He smiled. 'That will not be necessary.'

We all rose to our feet, and she gazed up at him with a grin, and made a little movement of her hips. 'Or anything else you might want,' she added with a wink, as she left.

Holmes closed his eyes in silent distress.

After Mrs Collett had gone, I said, 'Are you really going to try and find her husband's remains? The river police have not found anything in the last six weeks.'

'Consider this,' said Holmes. 'If I can discover any evidence to suggest that the torso is that of Mr Collett and not Mr Cloudsdale, then the charge of accessory to murder against Emmett will have a far stronger defence. It will raise the possibility that Mr Cloudsdale is not deceased. Also, any mistake in the prosecution case could be used to cast doubts on the whole. It is a slight hope, but it is all we have, and I must pursue it. I will start with the place of Mr Collett's employment and then the public houses. The conversation of hearty working men over their beer may furnish some clues as to when he was last seen. Intoxication is a great loosener of tongues.'

'I hope you are going in disguise,' I said.

'Naturally I will not announce myself to be a detective, or I will be told nothing,' said Holmes. 'I flatter myself that I can mingle convincingly in most levels of society, and this will be an ideal opportunity to observe and learn from the banter in a public house.'

I knew better than try and dissuade him. All I could reasonably do was express my concern as to the dangers of this proceeding. The reputation of the docklands even after so many new industries had been established, lingered on. Who knew what crimes were being carried out or planned in such surroundings? If Holmes was suspected of being a detective or a police informant, it might be his body stuffed into a bag weighted with iron and stones, waiting to be found at the bottom of the Thames.

CHAPTER TWENTY-TWO

I didn't see Holmes for several days after that conversation. I assumed that he had been working diligently on his impersonation of a labouring man before plunging into the beer dens of the Bermondsey wharves. I hoped he would be successful as he would be asking questions about a missing man and might possibly even be addressing the very man who had murdered him. Collett might still be alive, of course. Perhaps he had found a second wife and hoped the first one would not send someone to look for him. I could see that Holmes did not have any liking for Mrs Collett. His fastidious nature meant that he was appalled and repelled by such obvious coarseness in a woman, but I thought that she was far from being a bad person. Mrs Collett was a plain-speaking, hardworking wife, with a genuine sense of duty towards her missing husband.

There were times in those early days when it was useful for Holmes to have a neglectful landlady who took very little notice of what her tenants did or what visitors they entertained. Holmes was often back and forth from his Montague Street lodgings in different disguises. She might have suspected he was the head of a criminal gang, the members of which visited him for instructions, and preferred to remain ignorant of his activities. In later years, at Baker Street, Mrs Hudson was a jewel of understanding and discretion. My own landlady, who was used to medical students, the house in Farringdon being so near to Barts, had a suspicious eye, but I don't think I ever offended her.

My days were well employed catching up on my studies, but I made sure to let Mycroft know what Holmes was about. He too was worried, but accepted that there was nothing he could do, and promised to call in regularly at Montague Street in case there was any news. I called there once and learned that neither Holmes nor anyone vaguely resembling him had been there recently. I guessed that he had immersed himself thoroughly into the life of wharf side Bermondsey, which meant finding such basic accommodation as would protect him from the elements, perhaps doing some daily labouring work, and pretending to be foolish or inebriated, while listening to incautious talk.

The chief trade in Bermondsey in those years was the tanning of leather. Many such industries, the kind which produced noise and bad odours, were thought to be too offensive for the commercial City side of the river and had found a home there. Sawmills, soap-makers, tarpaulin-makers and lard refineries were all welcomed in Bermondsey. They clustered closely in narrow streets and insanitary yards which were frequently flooded by the outpourings of tanneries or the contents of bad drains. It was hard to lead an honest life in such surroundings, and the temptation of easy pickings from petty crime was constantly present.

I was at home, surrounded by my books and papers when I received a telegram from Mycroft. It read: 'Come to Montague Street at once.' I abandoned my work immediately and ran out to seize the first cab I could find, half afraid of what I might find.

I was relieved to see Holmes alive and conscious, although he was badly battered and exhausted. By the time I arrived, Mycroft had removed his brother's bloodied clothing, washed him down and towelled him dry. Holmes was slumped in an armchair enveloped in a warm dressing gown and woollen shawl over his pyjamas, before a newly made-up fire, clutching what smelled like a hot brandy laced with a little cocoa. There was a plate of bread and meat beside him into which he had already made substantial inroads. I had never seen him marked so heavily by combat, even from the boxing ring. Both his eyes were blackened, his cheekbones were bruised and there was a cut on the bridge of his nose.

'They do not abide by the Queensberry Rules in the public houses of Bermondsey,' said Holmes drily, when he saw my stares. 'But if you face them without fear and give a fair account of yourself you will earn their respect.' Mycroft had brought out such medical materials as were available, and I did what I could for my friend's abrasions, concerned that they might be concealing broken bones. I was obliged to consider Holmes's tendency to make light of injuries and made certain not to dismiss any suspicions of deeper trouble on his word alone. Fortunately, Holmes's sparring instructor was a practical man, a former fighter in the days of the old bare-knuckle bouts, who knew that not all combat is fair. Holmes was by far his best amateur student and this training had enabled him to deflect the power of body blows from ungloved fists, suffering only bruises rather than cracked ribs.

'I hope you learnt something that was worth all this trouble,' said Mycroft.

'I believe I did,' said Holmes. 'The drinkers at the various public houses are unable to provide a precise date on which they last saw Mr Collett, only that no-one could recall having seen him recently. But some said he might have got himself mixed up in something. Collett had mentioned that a trunk had been deposited in Mr Roberts' warehouse by two men, about which he had had some suspicions.'

'Was that because of a smell?' I asked.

'No, it appears that Mr Collett has no sense of smell,' said Holmes. 'Which explains a great deal. He was suspicious because the men who deposited it were concerned that it should be left undisturbed and were happy to pay above the usual rate for it. Also, there had been a number of robberies recently, from warehouses storing high-priced imported goods such as drugs and spices. Collett suspected that these men were responsible and were hiding stolen property from the police, hoping to dispose of it when the enquiry cooled a little. It seems that Mr Roberts, whose business methods must entail a lack of curiosity about what he stores for his customers, did not share his employee's concern. Collett had his eye on a possible reward and told his friends he was going to try some of the old keys in the scrap metal pile at the warehouse and see if any of them fitted the trunk.'

'Do you know if he did?'

'I believe he made the attempt. His friends told me that when they next saw him, they had asked him, in jocular fashion, if he had found any treasure in the trunk, and he admitted that while one or two keys fitted the lock, he had yet to find one that would turn to open it. I decided to pay a visit to Mr Roberts' warehouse. It is a repository of second-hand furniture which he buys and sells. Collett was employed to work in the warehouse and drive the wagon. I pretended to look around as a customer. There is nothing of great value there, and people come and go as they please during the day although it is locked at night. Roberts also undertakes rag sorting and scrap metal collection.'

'I don't suppose he stores dead bodies?' I asked, not especially seriously.

'That is to be determined,' said Holmes. 'I asked if a Mr Collett worked there and Roberts told me that the last time he had seen him was about six weeks ago, on the afternoon of the Friday when he disappeared. Roberts was called away to a house to view some furniture and when he came back Collett was gone. He hasn't seen him since.'

'And the trunk?'

'It is still there. I had a look. It was well made, and there was no unusual odour. It is labelled with the name J. Jones. I examined it and commented that I thought it very substantial. I pretended that I had been looking for something of the sort, but Roberts said it was not for sale. He was warehousing it for a customer. It is secured by two locks. Roberts did not have the keys and did not know what was in it. There were some scratches in the metal of the locks which looked recent, possible signs that Collett had attempted to open the trunk with keys that did not fit. But there was something else. He had mentioned being able to insert but not turn a key. I saw, however, that it was impossible to open the locks with any kind of key, or even insert a key. They had been filled with gutta-percha.'

I was astonished. Gutta-percha was a rubber-like material extracted from a tree, which has numerous applications. I think they make walking sticks from it. In its softened form, once inserted into a lock and allowed to harden that lock would be useless.

'The conclusion is obvious,' said Mycroft. 'The locks must have been sealed after Collett's attempts to open them if it was noticed that someone had tried to break in. To render them useless is a significant development. That trunk was never intended to be opened in the usual way.'

'I have advised Lestrade that there is a trunk in Bermondsey that should be investigated,' said Holmes. 'Let us see what can be found. If nothing else, the Southwark police may solve a robbery and apprehend the thieves when they come to collect their booty.'

CHAPTER TWENTY-THREE

It was vital that the men who had deposited the trunk did not remove it before it could be examined, and to this end, Southwark constables were ordered to keep a careful eye on the area in case the robbers returned to collect their spoils. The following morning all the preparations were in place. Holmes and I accompanied Lestrade, a constable, and an inspector from the police station on Borough High Street, an Irishman called Fox, to the warehouse of Mr Roberts. Holmes was making deliberate efforts to move as he usually did without giving any hint of pain. His face, however, was still swollen, and he was obliged to mention the dangers of working as a secret detective. 'I hope you gave as good as you got, Mr Holmes,' said Lestrade.

Holmes smiled, albeit carefully. 'There are three men who will regret trying my mettle,' he said.

The warehouse was a squat two-storey building with crumbling brickwork and a slimy and unswept yard for wagons and horses. A painted sign listed the goods to be found within: furniture and fittings of every kind, chinaware, tools, rags, and scrap. House clearances were a speciality. There was a tariff for storage, and a fee for deliveries.

Mr Roberts was a scrawny scarecrow of a man, who appeared to have clothed himself from the rag pile. There was a faded round hat on his head from which protruded a tangle of dirty grey hair, but his eyes, deep set in darkly grooved features, were watchful and wary.

'What's this?' said Roberts suspiciously when he saw the little deputation approach the warehouse doors.

'I must ask to conduct a search of your premises,' said the inspector. 'I have received information that some stolen goods have been deposited here.'

Roberts shrugged. 'If they have, I don't know anything about it,' he said. 'My business includes storing boxes and cases of all kinds, and I wouldn't get any customers if I was to ask what was in them. Have you got a magistrates' order?'

Inspector Fox had come prepared. He took the document from his pocket and held it up before the warehouseman. Roberts, who had evidently seen orders of this kind before, capitulated and reluctantly allowed us in.

'You want to search the whole premises?' asked Roberts.

'Only if necessary. To begin with I want to examine the packing case deposited by a Mr J. Jones,' said Fox.

'The one Dick Collett wanted to break open? You can't go doing that without good reason.'

'Have you seen Collett recently?'

'No. And I don't know where he is, either. His wife's been round here troubling me and I told her the same.'

We followed Roberts to a cavernous hall, with numbered spaces marked out on the floor with paint, each containing its own jumble of luggage, old furniture, boxes, and barrels. In one space stood a large dome-topped steamer trunk. Judging by the dents and scratches on its exterior, and the faded remains of old shipping labels, it must have seen the world a number of times before being pressed into simpler use. Its body was composed of stout wood, stained very dark, strengthened crossways by lighter staves secured by rivets, and bound with metal banding at the corners. The lid was fastened by two brass locks and there were carrying handles at either end.

'Who brought it in?' asked Holmes.

'Jones and his friend. It's a good weight. I fetched a trolley for them,' said Roberts. He suddenly stared at Holmes with a curious expression. 'You were here the other day, weren't you? Looking at the same trunk. Someone explain to you about being too nosey, did they?'

'Now then, that's enough of that,' said Lestrade, bending down to examine the locks. 'Was it you who sealed the locks? They appear to have been blocked with something.'

Roberts looked startled. 'No, and they weren't sealed when it was brought in. Jones had the keys, and he tested the locks to be certain they were secure.' He bent down and peered into the locks, then straightened up with a puzzled expression. 'I haven't done it, and I can't see why Collett would. It must have been Jones.'

'But you said they weren't sealed when it was brought in. Did anyone come back to inspect it?'

'Yes, that's right. Jones came and took the trunk away for a day and then brought it back again. It's his property and his business what he does with it.'

'Do you have a record of when the trunk arrived and its subsequent movements?' asked the inspector.

'I have a book, yes. The wife keeps it.'

'I would like to see it.'

Roberts walked to the rear of the hall, where a wooden enclosure housed a small office in which a woman sat at a desk writing in some ledgers. 'Martha, get us the book of deliveries for last month!' She put down her pen and was selecting the required book from a shelf when Roberts returned to us.

'So,' said Inspector Fox. 'This trunk. I want it opened. We can either open it up here or take it down to the station.'

'Break the locks, you mean?' said Roberts. 'Mr Jones won't like that.'

'That will be Mr Jones's lookout,' said the inspector. 'If he is sealing up keyholes it is a very suspicious action, and he has only himself to blame.'

'I'm not paying for the damage!' said Roberts.

'That is to be determined,' said Fox imperturbably. 'Kindly fetch me a crowbar.'

Roberts slunk away and as we waited, Martha brought us the book showing the dates on which the trunk had been deposited, taken away briefly, then returned. Holmes made careful notes.

'I have been informed that a number of robberies have taken place recently from warehouses storing high-priced goods. When did these robberies occur?' he asked.

'There's been a spate of them these last two months,' said the inspector. 'Very organised. The thieves know exactly where the valuables are, and how to get in and out of the most secure establishments. I think they put their own men in there, so they can work from the inside, leave windows unlocked, throw meat to any guard dogs. Not so much round here, but in the big warehouses at the main docks there'll be ivory, spices, drugs, cigars, silk. Some of these commodities are worth more than their weight in gold. And a clever thief knows how to pick and choose the best.'

Roberts returned with the crowbar. 'If it's his own property inside, Mr Jones will want compensation,' he said. 'I'll tell him the police are paying.'

The inspector and the constable between them began to prise open the lid of the trunk, the slightly battered material allowing the crowbar to be forced like a wedge between the domed top and the body. After both men leaned their weight on the solid iron implement, there was a cracking sound as the wood gave way and first one lock then the other was freed.

The lid was thrown open, and we peered in, but all we saw was a sheet of board fitting into the cavity of the packing case and sealed around the edges. 'Gutta-percha, I reckon,' said the inspector, 'the same as in the locks. That's easy to come by round here. A lot of the industries use it for insulating cables, coating wires and tarpaulins.' He found some purchase around the edge of the board, levered it up and removed it. Underneath was the smooth shine of a tarpaulin enclosing something.

The inspector placed a hand on the wrapping, sensing the shape and firmness of what was inside. Then he took his hand away and stepped back. 'I have a funny feeling what kind of thing this might be,' he said. 'And I don't think it's going to be spices.' He glanced at Holmes and me. 'You two are medical students, yes?'

We assented.

'Then let's take a look.' The tarpaulin was bound with a thick knotted cord, and the inspector's pocketknife not being strong enough for the task of cutting it, he sent Mr Roberts to fetch the sharpest knife he could find. Roberts, who could see where the enquiry was going, quite suddenly became more obliging. Once the cord was sawn through and the edges of the tarpaulin drawn aside, the odour left us in no doubt about the nature of its contents. The only question was identity. We were faced with what looked like the curve of a human arm, the flesh much discoloured, on which we could make out a crude tattoo which resembled a heeled boot.

Roberts, his voice muffled behind a soiled kerchief clutched to his face, uttered an oath. 'That's Collett,' he said. 'I'd know that tattoo anywhere. It's a map of Italy. He said his people were from there.'

'Do we have all of him, or only part, I wonder?' said Inspector Fox. 'Well, this isn't the place to determine that.' He restored the board to the trunk and closed the lid. 'I'll get this taken to the mortuary and call a surgeon.'

Roberts made no objection when the inspector commandeered a trolley and one of his horse-drawn wagons to remove the trunk. I think he was glad to see it go. It took all three policemen, assisted by Roberts, to load it onto the wagon. In view of the weight, I wondered what stolen booty might lie underneath, the discovery of which had got Collett killed for his curiosity. Having seen only one arm, I could not be sure how much of Collett might be in the trunk. Were there more remains waiting to be discovered elsewhere?

Inspector Fox ordered his constable to drive one of Roberts's traps to Southwark police station to fetch a surgeon and convey him to the mortuary, adding that once this was done, he should visit the Tooley Street tripe-shop to inform Mrs Collett of the discovery. Fox must have encountered Mrs Collett before, as he reassured the constable that she was unlikely to faint at the news. Lestrade, meanwhile, was deputed to remain at the warehouse and obtain from Roberts all the information in his possession about Jones and his friend, before joining us at the mortuary.

The nearest mortuary was at St Olave's Church, in Tooley Street, where it had been constructed very recently in the churchyard. It was not the height of perfection any doctor could have wished, but it was fit for purpose, properly equipped and ventilated, and a lot better than Millbank. I was pleased to learn that Southwark surgeons were not obliged to use their own handkerchiefs in the absence of towels.

On our arrival at the mortuary Inspector Fox called upon Holmes, me, and the keeper to help him manhandle the trunk

152

inside. I observed Holmes wincing a little, but he refused to admit to suffering any pain from his bruised ribs. Soon afterwards, the police surgeon, Dr Grice, bustled in and started to arrange things to his liking. He was brisk and efficient, and we thought it best to stand back and observe him work. We introduced ourselves as students at Barts Medical College, after which he viewed us with a more friendly air, and asked us to take notes for him, and assist if required. The post-mortem began.

CHAPTER TWENTY-FOUR

Although Collett must have been dead for several weeks, the sealed container in which his remains were stored had, while preventing the escape of odours and fluids which might have aroused suspicion of the contents of the trunk, also had the effect of slowing the process of decomposition. The remains were therefore in far better condition than an exposed body of the same age, although now it had been opened to the air, the process of decay was about to make up for lost time.

Grice lifted out the tattooed arm, and laid it on the table, and I admired the care and delicacy of his handling. Delving into the wrappings, he brought out another arm, this one bearing a tattoo of a five-pointed star. It was only later that I was told this is an ancient symbol of Italy, which further confirmed the identification of the remains.

'And we have a head,' he said, triumphantly, 'in good condition, too. Some assistance, please.' I stepped forward, since this required additional support to ensure this vital item was extracted as completely as possible. As we lifted it, I saw that thick dark hair and a moustache were still attached and the bitten ear mentioned by Mrs Collett was clearly visible, then my fingers encountered something unusual.

'There is a large depression at the back of the skull,' I said. 'A significant injury, with multiple fractures.'

We placed it gently on the table between the tattooed shoulders. I peered into the trunk to see what else was there. All that remained was the body below the waist. It was entire, but folded at the hips and knees, and once again I helped Dr

Grice in the removal and arrangement in respect to the other parts.

'Mrs Collett told us her husband had a bad foot,' I commented. One of the corpse's feet was of normal shape, but the bones of the other were distorted from what I thought was a defect he had endured since birth, and a brace or special boot would been required to enable him to walk with ease.

'But he must have had a torso,' said Inspector Fox drily. 'Where is that, I wonder?'

'A torso was found under Lambeth Bridge the other week,' said Grice. 'If it is unburied, I would like to see it. If buried, we may have to exhume.'

'That was identified as Mr Cloudsdale,' said the inspector.

'But only by his shirt and cufflink,' said Holmes. 'And Mrs Collett was adamant that it was her husband's.'

'Ah,' said the inspector. 'I'll see if it can be brought here. Dr Grice, are you sure all the remains we have here are from the same body?'

'I think so, yes. But once we have the torso and can match it to the severed limbs and head, I will be certain. There are more than enough distinguishing features for identification.'

'When the torso was found, Surgeon Bond said he believed the severing of the limbs and body had not been done by a medical man, but someone used to that kind of work,' said Holmes. 'This appears very similar.'

Grice nodded. 'I agree. We are of course in a location more than usually provided with slaughterhouses.'

As we considered this, the constable arrived with Mrs Collett. For once she was quiet as she gazed at the sections of the body on the table. She nodded. 'That's my Dickie,' she said. 'I can get him buried once he is all put together. How did he die?'

'There is a large, depressed fracture on the back of the skull,' said Grice. 'If he had suffered that when alive, it would have been a fatal injury.'

'Accident, or murder?' demanded Mrs Collett.

Holmes was making an examination of the skull, sketching the shape and position of the injury in his notebook. 'Narrow and longitudinal,' he said. 'He was struck by some kind of heavy implement, probably metal, rather than wood, given the extent of the damage. The angle of the injury suggests that the weapon was wielded by a right-handed man, some three to six inches taller than the deceased. Mr Collett was murdered.'

'I don't suppose anyone has a crowbar?' said Grice.

'You mean?' exclaimed the inspector.

'Only that now we have extracted the body, there is another board, very like the one on top, and also glued into the interior of the trunk with gutta-percha. I want to see what is underneath.'

'Mr Roberts has a crowbar,' said Holmes. 'I suggest the constable goes to fetch it. It might be the murder weapon.'

While we waited, Mrs Collett thanked Holmes for finding the body. She had studied his bruised face and was in no doubt that he had been injured on her behalf. 'I'll just say one thing,' she added. 'If the villain who killed my Dickie is ever found, and I think you are the man to find him, I want the law to let me interview him very closely, in some place where we wouldn't be seen or heard. Just for a few minutes. That's all.' She then went to commence the arrangements for a funeral.

When the crowbar was brought, it was studied with great care, but if it had been used to kill Collett there were no obvious marks or stains that would assist our case. It did, however, perfectly match the shape of the head wound. The inspector levered up the second board, hoping to see a cache of stolen valuables, but instead there was another ominous-looking shape encased in a tarpaulin. The cord that tied it was cut and Grice peered inside. 'Gentlemen,' he said, 'it appears we have another body, and this one is whole.'

It was a sad moment in more than one respect. None of us had ever met Anthony Cloudsdale, but Holmes, his brother and I had been living for some time with the faint hope that he would be found alive and be able to exonerate Emmett. He was a robust but not bulky man, in full health, showing the development that came with regular exercise. He had not been dismembered, merely folded up in a crouching position. It was not easy to lift him out, but we managed it, Holmes and I both lending our hands to the doctor, slowly and with great care and respect. We placed the body on another table, Grice guiding us as we worked as to the best means of doing so. Extending the limbs in order to make a proper study of the remains was something Grice wished to supervise very carefully. The body was unclothed, apart from a few fragments of underlinen. Anything which might have prevented it from being folded and pushed into the base of the trunk had been removed. But it was Cloudsdale. We saw the scar on the knee and the wart on the nose.

'I cannot arrive at a cause of death until I have made a full examination,' said Grice. 'There are no obvious external injuries.'

Lestrade had arrived and was there to witness the discovery. He too was saddened at the sight and said he would undertake to give Mrs Cloudsdale the news. He had completed his interview of Roberts, and while he thought that the warehouse business was an ideal one for criminals who wanted to store stolen goods and no questions asked, he did not think that Roberts had been involved in either of the murders. It was possible that Collett had been killed at the warehouse on his last day working there, during the time when Roberts was not on the premises, the body then taken to some nearby location for dismemberment. He had the name and address of the man Roberts had gone to see on that day and expected to have the alibi confirmed. Roberts had provided him with a full description of the mysterious Mr Jones who had left the trunk and his friend, which matched very well with that of MacBrian and his associate John. They had not given an address.

We had now established that the trunk had first arrived at the warehouse on the evening of the Tuesday after Cloudsdale's disappearance. It had been taken away on the morning of the Saturday following the last known sighting of Collett, and brought back later that day, accompanied by another item, a much smaller wooden crate, left to be called for. Jones had come to take the crate away on the day before the torso was discovered under Lambeth Bridge.

Although Grice had not yet seen the Lambeth Bridge torso, Lestrade, Holmes and I had a brief conference and we agreed that once it was brought to St Olave's and laid on the table with the remains of Dick Collett, it would make a complete body.

CHAPTER TWENTY-FIVE

Holmes was visibly shaken by our discovery of Mr Cloudsdale's corpse. Leaving Grice to his work, we hastened to see Mycroft at his club and revealed to him what had occurred. It was not often that I saw Holmes so low in spirits, as he reviewed how his well-intentioned actions had rebounded disastrously.

'It was my intention when making my enquiries in Bermondsey, to discover what had happened to Mr Collett in order to prove that the torso found was his and not that of Cloudsdale,' said Holmes. 'I thought by so doing I would preserve our hope that Cloudsdale was still alive and weaken the case against Joshua Emmett. Instead, we have the worst possible outcome from my labours, proof that Cloudsdale is dead, and most probably murdered since his body has been concealed. Also, the description of the men who deposited the trunk match the description of MacBrian and John, the very men who mentioned Emmett by name. MacBrian could well be Collett's murderer. This is the first indication we have that the two deaths are in any way connected. It can hardly be a coincidence.'

Mycroft struggled to accept the new findings. 'I will not believe even for a moment that Emmett can have inflicted violence on another individual. He would not harm a fly. If he was involved in concealment of a body, it would only have been under the most severe duress.'

'I accept your judgement of his character,' said Holmes. 'The only way to advance our enquiry now is to re-examine the facts in great detail and establish the sequence of events. Is there anything that might assist Emmett which we have missed?'

Mycroft was lost in thought, and I did not wish to launch the analysis, so Holmes began.

'We know that there is a gang of criminals: Yates, MacBrian, John, and a woman too. There may well be others. They must carry out many kinds of schemes, using locations they find convenient, certainly all over the capital, and possibly even further afield. They may use a place briefly and then abandon it and move on as it suits them. Their planning is meticulous. They will have places and materials arranged well in advance. Should an unexpected obstacle appear, they can take rapid action to counteract it. The gang is composed of men with specific expertise, as well as the foot soldiers and messengers. Controlling them is an intelligence, a planner. It may be that MacBrian is that controller.

'Sometimes, even the best schemes will fail, and I think in the case of Mr Cloudsdale it did, and it did so because they failed to read his character. To the corrupt, all men may appear to be corruptible, but that is not the case.

'Given the trouble they took, it must have been a long-term enterprise, with the intention of building a valuable asset for the future. They opened their campaign in a small way, working on what they considered to be Cloudsdale's weaknesses: his sense of duty, his loyalty to the Crown, his unquestioning trust in his superiors, his devotion to his family and, dare I say it, his readiness to answer the appeal of a young lady who begged assistance.'

'The lady with the yellow flowers in her hat?' I asked.

'Yes, she was where it began. She could also have been the veiled lady at the police court. It was essential to start with a scheme that would appear to be a worthy act, one sanctioned by his superiors but to be carried out in secret to conceal it from enemy agents. I have been given to understand that young ladies can be most persuasive in the case of gentlemen who are past their youth. The intention was that once Cloudsdale had carried out what was required, the demands would continue, and become greater. Before long, he would find himself unable to extricate himself and exposed to the danger of ruin if he did not comply. He would have been wholly in their power.'

Mycroft nodded sagely but did not comment.

'But they underestimated him,' Holmes continued. 'He began to see through the deception, possibly even realised that Yates was involved, and threatened to expose their activities. The gang members might have feared that if Yates was arrested, he might try and save himself by informing on them. It would have been a catastrophe. Cloudsdale had to be stopped, and quickly, before he could reach his office in Whitehall. Thus, the attempt on his life at Stepney was carried out as an emergency. But it failed. At least they knew where Cloudsdale must be bound — he was returning directly to Whitehall to tell his masters. Somewhere along the way, where we do not as yet know, he was waylaid, and killed. It took a little time to accumulate what was required to conceal the body. He might have died on the Monday, and by Tuesday all was in place.

'His body was placed in a trunk wrapped in a tarpaulin, the intention being to dispose of it when a suitable opportunity arose. Roberts's warehouse was an ideal place to store a trunk as he was not in the habit of asking questions if he was paid well. They may have used it before.'

'What of the shirt and the cufflinks?' I asked.

'The body would have been stripped of garments to make it easier to fold into the trunk. The clothes and cufflinks had some value, of course. There was a watch — that has not yet appeared. Most likely pawned. But the criminals had not anticipated Mr Collett's suspicions that there were stolen goods in the trunk, and hoping to discover more, he was trying unsuccessfully to open it. Unfortunately, his tongue loosened by drink, he mentioned this endeavour, and must have been overheard. Although he had not yet discovered a key to fit the lock, there was a danger that somewhere in the scrap metal pile he would find one.'

'Ah, I see your line of reasoning,' said Mycroft. 'The police were already taking the disappearance of Cloudsdale very seriously. It would be an advantage to have a body found that could be identified as his, preferably somewhere with no connection to Bermondsey. They didn't have a body but given the danger posed by Collett, they decided to use him.'

'Precisely,' said Holmes. 'He was similar in height and general build. They might have hoped to dress him in Cloudsdale's clothes, disfigure the face, and have him identified as Cloudsdale, but they reckoned without the numerous identifying marks they discovered on Collett's body. So, when Collett was killed, he was dismembered. The head, arms and legs would not have matched Cloudsdale, but the torso might if it was sufficiently decomposed and accompanied by Cloudsdale's possessions. It was wrapped in the shirt together with the cufflink and held somewhere — I suspect the smaller packing crate in the warehouse, probably well wrapped in a tarpaulin to avoid the smell of decomposition — until the time came to take it across the river and dispose of it under Lambeth Bridge. The ruse worked. The torso was thought to be that of Cloudsdale, and the river police were occupied searching for remains which were not there.'

'Why only the one cufflink?' I asked. 'And how did the other one come into the possession of Emmett? We were there when it was found. It was in his pocket.'

Holmes and Mycroft looked at each other and said nothing.

As I have already recorded, in my last meeting with Miss Jessup I had been greatly affected by the power of her emotions. Since then, I had been revolving in my mind the circumstances of the case against Joshua Emmett, and the time had not been unproductive. In fact, some thoughts had occurred to me which I hardly dared say, but now they bubbled to my lips.

I gathered my courage. 'Gentlemen,' I said. 'I hope you will not be offended but I do have some observations.'

'Please feel free to speak,' said Holmes. He turned to Mycroft. 'My associate often has his own viewpoints on my cases which, while rarely offering a solution, have been known occasionally to provide something of value.'

That was the most appreciation I was likely to receive. Holmes bowed his head, resting his chin on his chest in contemplation. Mycroft did nothing to conceal his scepticism. I cleared my throat. 'Sir,' I said to Mycroft, 'you have known Mr Emmett for many years, and I am sure you judge him correctly. You cannot imagine him as a criminal, or a willing accomplice. But the weight of evidence that has accumulated around him troubles you. This is your explanation. Emmett has been drawn into something in much the same way Cloudsdale was, something that had all the appearance of being lawful, even virtuous, and might if carried out efficiently have advanced his career. He made a solemn oath never to disclose what he knows. But now it must appear to him that the scheme was not what he had been led to believe, so why does he still say nothing? Your answer is that there is a strong reason he cannot break that oath. Some of the circumstances he may be unable to explain — they might have been kept a secret from him. For the rest he fears that if he reveals what he knows he may be killed — not an idle threat as we now know — or worse still, those he loves will be harmed. All he can do to protect them is to stay silent.'

Mycroft nodded. Holmes merely leaned back in his chair with a suspicious glint in his eye.

I took a deep breath. 'What I am proposing is you may both be mistaken.'

I waited for the brothers' reaction. My biggest fear was not humiliation, but that this would mark the end of my friendship with Sherlock Holmes.

CHAPTER TWENTY-SIX

There was a chilly silence. 'Continue,' said Holmes at last.

'You have said to me many times, that in the solution of a mystery emotion has no place. It can mislead, distract. You collect the facts; you evaluate them for their significance and discard those that have none. What remains are the pieces which give order to the situation and lead you inexorably to the solution. But when we last spoke to Miss Jessup, when we heard of her demeanour on visiting Emmett after his arrest, I was forcibly struck by her unwavering belief in his complete innocence. Yes, she loves him, he is the man she wants to marry and spend her life with. Yes, she is distraught by what has happened and cannot imagine that he has ever done anything wrong. Therefore, Miss Jessup believes that Emmett is hiding nothing. He says nothing because he knows nothing. She is convinced that when he tells us he cannot reveal what he knows because he is as mystified as we are, it is because he is telling the truth. He has been telling the truth right from the beginning.'

I saw the two brothers exchange glances.

Mycroft shook his head and answered me as if addressing a child. 'Women are emotional, intuitive creatures,' he explained. 'They do not have the higher levels of logical thought that men do. That is all very well in its place, there are spheres of life in which intuition has a value, but here — I really don't think —' he sighed. 'There are far too many pieces of evidence all pointing the same way, and none to support your suggestion.'

'All I ask,' I said, 'is that you reconsider the evidence in the light of Miss Jessup's belief. Start your deliberations with the assumption that she is right. Who knows, something new might appear.'

Mycroft was unconvinced, but I saw that Holmes was more engaged.

'I am not saying we should embrace this theory,' said Holmes, 'but it might produce something useful if we were to treat it as an exercise of the intellect. Let us, for the sake of argument, adopt Stamford's suggestion that Emmett is being truthful and see if any of the circumstances of the case may admit of a different explanation.'

'But there is too much to simply explain away!' exclaimed Mycroft. 'Not all of it can be coincidence or chance. And I can't believe the villains are placing blame on Emmett to distract from the real culprits. Why Emmett? He has led a blameless life. He has no enemies. He cannot be an obvious scapegoat, a believable criminal. It makes no sense at all.'

'Nevertheless,' said Holmes, looking comfortable and lacing his long pale fingers, 'let us commence the exercise.'

Mycroft shrugged. 'Very well. Where do you want to begin?'

'Let us start with the lady with the yellow flowers in her hat. What is her function?'

'A courier,' said Mycroft. 'Passing messages, giving an air of friendliness that might draw in a man who is susceptible to that kind of female.'

'Why the yellow flowers?'

'To make her recognisable to a stranger when conducting secret meetings or exchanging documents.'

'She might,' said Holmes, 'have chosen just one or two flowers, but instead she wore a spray of them which made her look distinctive from a distance. To Mrs Cloudsdale's cousin Hilda for example. And was it chance that she chose the very article in which Miss Jessup is adept? The making of silk flowers? Emmett might not have noticed her hat when she dropped her parcels in the street, but Miss Jessup was sure to.'

'But how could she have known of Miss Jessup's special interest in making silk flowers? They had never met,' objected Mycroft.

'Secret observation, perhaps. The lady is a spy,' said Holmes, but neither brother appeared convinced by this argument.

'You are saying that she wanted to be noticed?' asked Mycroft. 'And not in any subtle way.'

'That might be the case. Recall the yellow paper flower she gave to the delivery boy. A small detail but effective. Its function was to link the Cloudsdale disappearance with the payment. A payment made the day after the secret meeting attended by Emmett, which was the same day that the trunk containing Cloudsdale's body was delivered to Mr Roberts's warehouse.'

'How could she have known we would find the boy?' Mycroft objected.

'She did not, but if we had not done so he might have been urged to come forward.'

'The manager of the tea shop, Mr Bradley,' said Mycroft. 'He said he had seen Emmett walking with her in the park.'

'Which Emmett denies, absolutely,' I interposed. 'Mr Bradley could be mistaken or lying.'

'Emmett's defence should offer that suggestion,' said Holmes. 'Mr Ineson did think the man would not perform convincingly in court. Has this unexpected witness received any payments recently? We should find out.' He stroked his chin thoughtfully. 'I have been wondering if the veiled lady we saw in court was our messenger, only wearing a different, less noticeable hat. I feel sure I have heard her voice before. She was not, I think, dressed as a lady then…' Holmes mused for a while, then snapped his fingers. 'Yes! I have it! You have seen her too, Stamford, in the high court, the witness box, very simply clad. Her words sent a man to the gallows. If I am right, that woman has a heart like ice. She will sacrifice anyone for her own ends. She might appear to be a minor player in the game, but that is what makes her so dangerous.'

'And the fifty-pound note Emmett received?' asked Mycroft. 'That is not an inconsiderable sum.'

'Any less would not have attracted as much attention,' said Holmes. 'It appeared to be payment for an important favour.'

'Which Emmett denies.'

'Indeed.'

'I must say,' said Mycroft, 'if I wished to inconvenience a man, the last thing I would do is send him a fifty-pound note.'

'Unless it implicated him in a serious crime that he knew nothing about,' said Holmes.

Mycroft grunted. 'I am still not convinced. Well, go on.'

'Let us turn to the events as reported by Emmett on the day after Cloudsdale's disappearance. He could not have taken part in the abduction as he was at his desk, but on the day after, he had time, more than two hours, for which he cannot convincingly account. He can produce not one shred of proof of where he was. A paper which is no longer in his possession. A house with an empty room which he was unable to find later on. We have assumed either that he was mistaken as to the place or was lured away from his desk so his papers could be searched. But suppose neither of those assumptions is correct.'

Mycroft said nothing, only made a little helpless gesture of his hands.

'Let us now, as Stamford has suggested, re-examine the story of that absence on the basis that Emmett has told the truth,' Holmes continued. 'To begin with, the note on official paper.

A forgery to ensure he is not at his desk at a critical time, so as to falsely incriminate him. He obeys the order, which appears to be an official direction, and goes to the address. He tells no-one, as instructed. He gives the note to the valet, who we now believe is a member of the gang. The description of the young man with pierced ears may or may not play in Emmett's favour. He is shown to the room which is set out as for a meeting. Told to wait, he is distracted, and his continued attendance at the scene for a suitable period of time is ensured by being asked to write an essay on an innocuous subject. Just as he becomes restless, he is told that the meeting has been postponed and he should go home and await further instructions. The next day he received fifty pounds.'

'But he said that the valet had the key to the apartment,' said Mycroft. 'The housekeeper Mrs Purdue told you that there are two, she has one and the tenant the other. And the valet must have had a front door key to go in and out of the house without the housekeeper's knowledge.'

'Unless the tenant, Miss Noone, is a gang member and simply lent her keys to the valet, or had copies made,' said Holmes.

'Another woman? How many are there?' demanded Mycroft.

'Let me see, the veiled lady, the lady with the yellow flowers in her hat, and Miss Noone. Just the one, I think,' said Holmes.

I could see Mycroft's cynicism wavering. 'The housekeeper may not be innocent in this,' he said.

'She cannot be ruled out as a participant,' observed Holmes.

'Did you learn anything from examining the vase?' I asked.

'From the vase, no, but the mantlepiece on which it stood had been cleaned and polished very recently.'

'The cufflink!' exclaimed Mycroft.

'There is a hall stand for visitors' overcoats and umbrellas on the ground floor,' said Holmes. 'Did Emmett hand his coat to the valet to be hung up? Was it the same one he wore when arrested? It was by then more than twenty-four hours from Cloudsdale's disappearance. The valet may well have had the cufflink in his possession and slipped it into Emmett's pocket.'

'He was singularly unlucky to have been wearing that same coat when Lestrade searched him,' I said.

'Was he?' Holmes queried. 'Does he have another?'

'But the photographer — MacBrian — he actually mentioned Emmett by name,' said Mycroft.

'He did, very clearly and his associate repeated it back to him, to make sure Mr Lambourn recalled it,' said Holmes.

'But how did MacBrian know Emmett's name?'

'That,' said Holmes, 'is the most interesting question of all.'

All three of us were for a time, lost in thought, but there was nothing further to discuss.

'These are certainly useful observations, and I shall advise Mr Ineson,' said Mycroft, eventually. 'If nothing else, they may produce some doubts in the minds of a jury.'

'My only concern,' said Holmes, 'is the number of times I have witnessed trials of men who are very obviously guilty and whose only defence is that all their accusers are lying. It is a very weak case, a case made by the desperate, without proof. It generally fails.'

'Then we must find proof, if there is any to be had,' said Mycroft. 'Where shall we begin?'

'The Bayswater lodging house,' said Holmes. 'We only saw the hallway and one room. There is more to see and if there is anything to support what Emmett says, it will be there.'

'But we have no authority to go there,' I said.

'A little ingenuity may be required,' said Holmes, a spark of mischief in his eyes. I thought he was contemplating an adventure in one of his many disguises, but the scale of what he was planning was not yet apparent.

CHAPTER TWENTY-SEVEN

'I hope,' I said to Holmes when we were next able to speak privately, 'that you are not contemplating breaking into the apartment in Bayswater?'

'Of course not,' said Holmes, 'and for a very good reason.'

'Because it is against the law?' I suggested.

He smiled. 'That would not hold me back if it was for the greater good — no, I simply do not have the skill. And if there is something there which would cast some light on past events, it would assist no-one for me to obtain it in that way. Any evidence must be seen in place by the police, or it has no value.'

'And how will you achieve that?'

'I will not burgle the apartment; I will simply make it appear that that is what has taken place. Once I have the materials I need to carry out my plan, I will advise you, since I will need your assistance.'

'Will your brother be assisting also?'

'No, he has his part to play but not in this business.'

He did not elaborate but I feared that the essential quality Mycroft lacked which I had, was the ability to run away very fast.

As Holmes was well aware, most crimes of burglary were clumsy affairs which involved breaking windows, forcing locks, and snatching valuables. A rapid entry and egress were essential, and almost always left a wake of damage and disarray. This was far from what interested and even attracted Holmes to that activity. There was another class of burglar, however; a skilled artisan, with a set of fine tools and delicacy of touch, who could pick locks, leaving no sign of his work. Such a burglar could enter a premises and abstract what he desired — jewellery perhaps, or important documents — and then silently be on his way, unsuspected, leaving no clues as to his identity. It would take long and patient hours of practice to achieve this level of expertise, one which Holmes would, in time, add to his armoury.

Holmes spent the next day carrying out some secret preparations in which I was not required to assist him, and the following afternoon a short note summoned me to his rooms. He still had the marks of his recent combat on his face, but these were fading, and he was moving more easily.

'What do you want me to do?' I asked.

'You may have noticed that the houses in that street are not one continuous terrace but a series of short ranges of terraced properties, divided from each other by narrow alleyways. These lead to open areas at the rear, where there are small gardens and gates to enable deliveries to be made to the kitchens and cellars. There are steps at the front leading down to a basement door. In the case of the house Emmett showed us, this door was strong and secure, with a brass knocker, and must be the entrance to the housekeeper's apartments. Any burglar would be ill-advised to attempt to enter the property from the street but would concentrate his efforts on the rear. Following what we saw of apartment number two, I made a sketch of the room and the position of the doors. I believe I can identify from the outside of the building the window a burglar might wish to use.'

'But you will not enter that way?'

'I will not enter the house at all.'

That was something of a relief, but when I asked for more detail Holmes was infuriatingly mysterious. 'The less you know the better,' he said. 'All I require of you this evening is to be at the front of the house and watch carefully to see if anyone rushes out. If someone does, make a note of their description and the direction in which he or she goes, but do not attempt to follow. You are simply a passer-by who has seen someone running away and you will report your sighting to the police. Even if you see no-one, you will, I can guarantee you, have heard something suspicious.'

'And where will you be?'

'I will be at the back, watching in case anyone flees that way.'

'Will there be police in the area?'

'Yes, Mycroft has ascertained the patrol times of the local police, and there is one constable, who is very regular on his beat. Given what transpired when we made our visit with Lestrade, I am not sure this officer is doing any more than keeping a watchful eye in passing. But I should be able to see when he is near enough to be alerted. I will advise you of when to take up your position. Please do not be late.'

Anyone who assists Holmes in his endeavours will find that much of his time is spent in awaiting terse instructions which are to be obeyed immediately and without question. In the early evening of the next day, I accordingly found myself lurking near to the house in Bayswater trying not to appear suspicious. How successful I was is a question I am unable to answer. It was after dark, but the street was well lit with gas lamps, and as the time approached, I was able to see the constable approaching.

As he drew near to the house there was a series of loud noises coming from the rear of the property, a crash as if some object like a wooden packing case had fallen to the ground, followed by the sound of breaking chinaware. The startled constable ran up and I hurried up too, pointing to the house. 'I think it came from there!' I exclaimed.

'Stay there, sir,' he said, and blew a number of blasts on his whistle. He then ran down the side alley. I did as I was instructed, and watched for anyone leaving the house, but no-one appeared. Before long the constable returned, and another had arrived on the scene. 'Looks like a burglary,' said the first constable to his associate. 'Fallen ladder and I think an upper window is open. Lots of broken china. No-one in sight. This man might have seen something.'

'I only heard a noise as I was passing,' I said. 'I didn't see anything.'

The second constable was writing in his notebook when the basement door opened and Mrs Purdue came out, having thrown a greatcoat around her shoulders. 'What's happening?' she demanded. 'What's all the noise?'

'We think someone has been trying to burgle the house,' said the first constable. 'If you don't mind, we would like to take a look around in case he is still inside, but I think it is probable he has run away. There is broken china at the back.'

'Oh no, my vases!' she exclaimed. And then, to my horror, Mrs Purdue saw and recognised me. 'I know that man!' she exclaimed, pointing a finger. 'He has been here before, poking his nose about with his criminal friends! One of them was arrested!'

'Did you now?' said the second constable, staring at me as if I was about to run away, which in fact I had a good mind to do. 'You seem to have got yourself in bad company. Looking things over for your burglar friends, were you?'

'I — no — I just happened to be passing by!' I protested.

'I think you had better come with us to the station. I'm sure the inspector will be interested to hear what you have to say.

You're not going to make this hard for yourself, are you?' he added, towering over me in a highly meaningful manner.

'No, no, of course not.'

There was nothing I could do but comply. I didn't know where Holmes was, and I could only hope he had got away. 'Sergeant Lestrade of Scotland Yard will vouch for me,' I said as I was marched along the road, the constable's enormous hand clamped about my upper arm. It was only about ten minutes or so, but I felt I was being paraded along the street like a condemned criminal. I had enough time to ruminate on my position, and what I ought to say when questioned, and managed to confuse myself so much that I eventually concluded that the less I said, the better. It was hard to decide whether the truth, which I could not reveal as it would implicate Holmes, or a weak lie I could not defend would get me into more trouble. My mood was not helped on arriving at Paddington police station on Harrow Road, a monstrous grey edifice which loomed over every other building like the walls of a prison. By the time I had been admitted, given my name, address and occupation, and placed in a cold, desolate little room awaiting interview, I feared that both my career and my reputation were in ruins.

CHAPTER TWENTY-EIGHT

My solitary thoughts were descending through pessimism in the direction of panic. I was struggling to think how I would explain this predicament to my parents, who have been so generous in supporting me during my student years. I was beginning to consider what prison sentence I might receive and what, if any, employment I would be able to find on release, when the door opened, and the constable peered in. 'Someone to see you,' he said.

To my surprise and relief, it was Mr Ineson, who sat beside me and examined some papers. 'Have you been questioned yet?' he asked, brusquely.

'No.'

'Have you said anything?'

'I think I might have said I was just passing, but that was all. And I said Lestrade would vouch for me.'

'Well, don't say anything else. Mr Holmes — Mr Mycroft Holmes that is, asked me to stand by in case of emergency, and told me to come here urgently. I had expected to find his brother here, but I think he is on his way. What has he been up to?'

'I — don't really know. He wouldn't tell me anything. But he said he had no intention of breaking the law.'

'That does not mean he did not do so,' said Ineson, wearily. 'Your ignorance of tonight's events, if genuine, may prove to be an advantage. Let me do the talking and try not to interrupt.'

I had a miserable wait, until a young inspector called Keating arrived in company with Lestrade and Holmes, who seemed not to have taken any harm from his adventures.

'We have examined the house for signs of burglary,' said Keating, 'and it appears that there have been no intruders in the building, and nothing has been taken. Some broken chinaware outside the house was not the property of any resident or the owner. An attempt may have been made to enter since a window has been left open, and a ladder which was probably propped against the wall, has fallen to the ground. But we have no evidence of who might have done this and what they were after. Mr Stamford, my constable has confirmed that you were not near the house when the noise was made. The police have an eye on you, but we have decided not to make any charges.'

My relief at this pronouncement was profound.

'I ought to mention, Inspector Keating,' said Lestrade, 'that Mr Holmes here has done valuable work for Scotland Yard in the past, examining scenes of crime for evidence, and Mr Stamford has assisted him. In view of what occurred this evening, I would like them to cast their eyes over the room which we think the would-be intruder made his target, in case there is anything of note.'

'It's somewhat irregular,' said Keating, 'but as you vouch for them, I will allow it. However, I will accompany you.'

Mr Ineson, seeing no further requirements for his services, took his leave, commenting only that his invoice would be in our hands very shortly.

We returned to the Bayswater house where Mrs Purdue was astonished to see me still at large. Inspector Keating had to be very insistent as to the requirement for us to examine the apartment, and it was with extreme ill-grace that she agreed to allow it. She conducted us upstairs, constantly glancing back at me with an expression of deep suspicion. She made no comment on Holmes's bruised features, but smiled in a satisfied manner, possibly suspecting that there had been a falling out amongst thieves.

The parlour was the same as before, clean and nicely arranged, with nothing apparently missing. Recalling Emmett's suggestion that the little table might have served as the desk he had used to write his essay, I removed the cloth and saw a plain wooden surface beneath. It had two shallow drawers, which contained cutlery. Holmes examined the surface of the table through his glass. 'The table has been used as a desk,' he said. 'A drop of ink on the surface has been cleaned, but there is a trace of it remaining in the grain of the wood.' He pointed out the place. 'Here, where it would have fallen from a pen held in the right hand of a man seated here.' Keating and Lestrade stared at the mark on the tabletop but did not comment.

There was nothing more to be learned from the parlour, and we were permitted at last to enter the adjoining room. This was a bedroom with a single bed, its covers undisturbed, a dressing table with brushes and combs, and a wardrobe containing ladies' clothes. All were carefully examined but nothing of interest emerged. Holmes searched underneath the bed and extracted a small trunk which was fastened by a padlock.

'That belongs to Miss Noone,' said Mrs Purdue. 'I don't have the key. I expect she has it with her.'

'It is a common type of lock,' said Holmes. 'You may already have a key that will fit.'

With noticeable unwillingness, Mrs Purdue searched her bundle of keys. There were several of the right size and type, and one of them was, with a little pressure, persuaded to open the trunk. This time there was no sealant of gutta-percha or bodily remains, but the contents told us a story. We found a packet of clean writing paper, an inkstand, a bottle of ink, pens and a blotter. We then lifted out and examined a set of cheap framed pictures of the kind that Emmett had described as having been in the room at the meeting. Most notably, one was a print of an ironclad, steam-driven warship with a single gun turret, named HMS *Kingston*. There was a crack in the lower right corner of the frame.

Lestrade at once saw the significance of this last item, and arrangements were made for the trunk and its contents to be removed to the police station. 'I don't know what has been happening here,' he said, 'but there might have been some mischief taking place or being planned. The writing materials are a common sort. The pictures are not of any value. I doubt if we will be able to discover who purchased them, but I suppose we must try.'

The sergeant clearly had something else on his mind which he wanted to discuss with us, but the presence of Inspector Keating prevented him from expressing himself. Once we had completed our work at the apartment he was able to talk to Holmes and me privately over some hot coffee at a nearby café. 'Now then, Mr Holmes,' he said, 'I am not going to ask you what you have been up to, since I am not sure you would tell me the truth, and if you did, I would not approve of the answer, and both of you would be in trouble. What I will say is that the new information now in our possession has been useful and I am not sure we would have got it by any other method. In my judgement it is best not to pursue the point.'

We acknowledged his decision without comment.

'I do have some news for you. As anticipated, the Lambeth Bridge torso once reunited with the limbs and head found in

Bermondsey was, according to Dr Grice, a perfect fit and we now have the complete body of Mr Collett. That and the body of Mr Cloudsdale have been formally identified, and the inquest adjourned for a full post-mortem.

'Also, I think from our records we can put a name to the young man who acted as an assistant to Mr MacBrian, and who from his description might well have been the same person who attempted to murder Mr Cloudsdale at Stepney station, and played the role of valet when Mr Emmett made his visit to the property at Bayswater. His name is John Clay, and he has been involved in crimes of all kinds from an early age, thieving and swindling and the like. On the few occasions he has been apprehended, he has put on airs and claimed he is of royal descent, demanding special treatment. If he is of royal descent, no noble family has been eager to claim him as their own. The pierced ears are what gave him away; he says they were done for him when he fell into the hands of gypsies. But given his nature one can hardly know what to believe. And now it seems he will not draw a line at murder.' Lestrade shook his head.

'We do know now that Joshua Emmett was telling the truth about being at the Bayswater address,' said Holmes.

'The evidence suggests as much,' said Lestrade, 'but we still have nothing to show when he was there, who else was present, and what took place. He is far from being exonerated, Mr Holmes.'

CHAPTER TWENTY-NINE

If Holmes was sorry that he had almost ended my career as a surgeon before it had begun, he did not say so. I did not reproach him, but neither did I vow never to do anything of the sort again. I always embarked on these adventures with anxiety, trepidation, and a touch of queasiness but somehow I survived them and never hesitated to take the plunge again. What that says about me, I really do not know.

'Perhaps now you can tell me what your plans were,' I said, when Lestrade had left us.

'Ah yes, the ladder and the chinaware,' he said. 'I had observed that the upper windows of the property were of the sash type, and thought that the lock might be teased open, and the lower portion raised quietly and without visible damage using a thin, strong knife. I undertook a little practice on my own windows until I felt sufficiently adept. Earlier in the day I took a ladder and a scalpel to the house and applied my new skills. I was able to raise the window just a little, enough to suggest that a slender person had gained access. I did not, of course, enter. I descended and laid the ladder on the ground, resting it against the wall below, where it lay hidden behind a few shrubs. When I came back in the evening, I raised the ladder and placed it against the wall under the window once more. When I knew the policeman was approaching, I pushed the ladder over to make a noise. I then broke some pieces of cheap china, which I had brought with me, to suggest that someone had tried to make away with the vases. I knew the noise would bring the constable running. I had not, however, anticipated his fellow constable arriving quite so soon afterwards, but one cannot always be precise about these things.'

'Did no-one notice you earlier in the day when you brought the ladder and climbed up it?' I asked.

'Apparently not. And Mrs Purdue ought to be grateful to me, since I left her windows in spotless condition and charged her nothing for the service.'

Mycroft joined us for the next consultation with Mr Ineson. The solicitor did not delve too deeply into the events that had led to my arrest, but he was impressed with what we had so far discovered, if not the methods we had employed to do so. His best hope for Emmett remained at putting enough doubt in the mind of a jury to weaken the prosecution case.

'We appear to have two situations which are intertwined,' said Ineson. 'Firstly, there is undoubtedly a criminal conspiracy to obtain valuable secret documents and sell them to the highest bidder. But the circumstances of this crime, serve, in addition, to incriminate my client, who I am obliged to believe is an innocent man, a man who continues to insist that he had no part at all in any crime, even as an unwitting dupe, or acting under duress. The evidence that purports to incriminate him is substantial and cannot be put down to mere chance. If we could discover a convincing motive for the attempts to incriminate Mr Emmett, something other than simply putting the blame on a convenient scapegoat, which is a vague and weak argument, his defence would be far stronger.' He turned to Mycroft. 'Can you suggest any reason at all why someone would wish to destroy Joshua Emmett? I have asked him if he is named in a will and due to inherit a fortune which would go to another man if his reputation was ruined, but he said that if that was the case, he knew nothing of it.'

'His family and connections are not wealthy,' said Mycroft. 'And regarding his position in government service; yes, he was hoping for a promotion, but it would not have been especially highly paid, just another small step in advancement, and well deserved. It would not have impeded the career of another man, or aroused jealousy.'

'Could it be jealousy of another kind?' asked Ineson. 'Concerning his recent engagement? I have known men to be murdered for that motive. Do you know if Miss Jessup has ever been betrothed to another, and thrown this man over to transfer her affections to Emmett?'

'I am quite sure there is nothing to find,' said Mycroft. 'They have known each other for several years. She was just sixteen when they met. Their friendship was almost immediate, and this quickly ripened into a sincere and devoted love. I do not think Miss Jessup has ever entertained a moment's thought of another man as her future husband. Emmett is her first and only sweetheart.'

'It is a delicate subject,' said Holmes, warningly.

'It is, but I am sure she would be open about it if she thought it would save him,' said Mycroft.

'What of Miss Jessup's expectations?' asked Ineson. 'There may be something she does not know about. A fortune that will come to her on reaching a specified age, or on marriage. If you agree, I can look into that possibility.'

'Please do,' said Mycroft. 'Nothing of that kind has been mentioned to me. I did take the opportunity of acquiring further information on that point. The Jessup family has never been rich, but once lived in comfortable circumstances until ten years ago when her father, who was in the construction business, suffered an accident, and their income has been consequently reduced. I believe he purchased a small annuity in better times, which keeps them from penury. He has a workbench at home where he carves wooden toys; Miss Jessup provides silk flowers and corsages for a company making fashionable evening costumes; and Mrs Jessup takes care of her husband, does a little needlework and all the work of the house.'

'There must be something we have failed to think of,' said Holmes. 'Something so heartless and wicked, so callous of human suffering that we can scarcely conceive of it. Even —' and here I saw his eyes widen. 'Horror upon horror, the acts of a man who is so deranged that he destroys others for no reason, solely for his amusement, simply because he can.' This concept was one of madness, beyond any form of logic, and it appalled Holmes, as something malevolently destructive and so covert and unpredictable that it might lie outside the scope even of his abilities.

When I next spoke to him alone, I saw that his thoughts had gone into a dreadful place. He had conceived of an evil so powerful, so untouchable, that it could only be fought by taking the law into his own hands and destroying it at the risk of his own life. Years later, Holmes as a mature detective was able to face these thoughts with equanimity and acceptance. For a youth of twenty-three, it was a hard concept for him to grapple with.

He was not idle in the coming days. I saw him scanning his vast collection of newspapers and cuttings, for reports that might lead him to the other gang members, any hint of criminal activity that had their stamp. Since Lestrade had already identified John Clay, the police were on the lookout for him. The lady with the yellow flowers in her hat was less easy to find. The hat or its trimming might have been burnt by now, and the lady herself — who was able to change her garments and appear in society as an anonymous shadow — would be hard to discover. The real mystery was MacBrian, of whom we had a description of sorts. He appeared to be the senior member of the gang and possibly its leader. Holmes believed that when Cloudsdale had left the Fenchurch Street workshop where the papers had been copied, to go to Stepney, with Clay chasing after him intent on murder, so MacBrian had taken the train going in the opposite direction, to Charing Cross. His intention was that if Clay should fail, he would try and intercept Cloudsdale before he could return to his masters in Whitehall. How MacBrian had achieved this and spirited the man away Holmes had still to discover, but a thought did cross his mind and he engaged Mycroft to make some further enquiries, in particular to establish if there was any chance that Cloudsdale had reached the office and left with anyone else. The results were surprising.

CHAPTER THIRTY

When we next met with Mycroft, he told us that despite all the enquiries he had made amongst men he knew well and trusted there was no evidence that Cloudsdale had returned to his office after delivering the envelope, and he had not been seen in the vicinity with another unidentified man. Given the sightings on the train, it was now looking probable that he had disappeared at some point on the short journey, just a few minutes' walk, from leaving the train at Charing Cross to Whitehall.

Mycroft had taken the opportunity of examining the hall porter's record books, which noted deliveries, arrivals, and departures. Drummond, whom we had seen giving evidence before the Westminster magistrates, had occupied his post at Whitehall for some twenty years, and was known for his reliability. He and his wife, to whom he had been married for fifteen years, and who cleaned the offices, lived in a small but comfortable apartment in the building. A recent addition to the porterage staff was Osmond, an active young fellow available to fetch and carry and take messages. He also manned the desk and kept the record books when Drummond went to take his meals.

Mycroft, on examining the books, was able to distinguish the entries signed off by Drummond, and a few with Osmond's initials. Drummond's mealtimes were generally predictable, but on the day of Cloudsdale's disappearance, there was an entry initialled by Osmond, relating to the arrival of some postal packets, at a time when Mycroft thought Drummond would normally have been on duty.

'I asked Osmond about the time of that entry, and he remembered the circumstances,' he told us. 'The police had also queried it and appeared to be satisfied with his explanation. According to Osmond, Drummond wasn't feeling quite himself, he said he had "a bout of the collywobbles" and thought he might have eaten something that disagreed with him. He had to go back to his rooms to rest. The police have interviewed Drummond and also Mrs Drummond who confirmed that her husband was in his rooms and obliged to lie down and rest because of "pains in his belly". Osmond told me that Drummond was only away for about an hour.'

'Any absence from duty at such a crucial time could be highly significant,' said Holmes. 'A period of an hour during which Drummond was not at his post, but with confirmation from Mrs Drummond as to where he was.'

'There was one signature of Osmond's on the books at 11.15 that morning, but no more of his that day,' said Mycroft. 'He said that Drummond returned to the desk shortly afterwards.'

'We only have Osmond's word that he was there the whole time,' said Holmes. 'Did anyone else comment on Drummond's absence, or see the desk unmanned?'

'Not to my knowledge,' said Mycroft.

'Just as Sir Crawford Yates, a man known to Cloudsdale, was able to divert him from his proper purpose, so either Drummond or Osmond could have done the same,' said Holmes. 'In fact, his fright that morning would have meant that he could not have been diverted by a stranger without the use of force, and there have been no reports of such an incident.'

'But how would either of the porters or anyone at Whitehall have known what had occurred only shortly before at Fenchurch Street?' I asked. 'What about Yates?'

'Yates was still at his luncheon,' said Holmes. 'The only possibility is that one of the porters is in the pay of the gang. If as we believe, MacBrian took the Charing Cross train while Cloudsdale was still on his way to Stepney, he would have had time to reach the offices well before his quarry arrived and give the alarm. He would have told someone he knew, someone who Cloudsdale trusted, about the new danger, and gave instructions as to what must be done.'

'One of the porters must have looked out for Cloudsdale and met him before he reached the office,' said Mycroft.

'I agree,' said Holmes. 'He was vulnerable, in a state of panic after the attempt on his life. He dared not go home in case he endangered his family. What would have diverted him? Perhaps he was told that his superiors already knew of his plight and had given orders that he must be taken to a place of safety and remain there for a while. He must have been promised that a note of explanation and reassurance would be delivered to his wife. Cloudsdale would not have gone with MacBrian, a man he now did not trust, but he would have gone with a Whitehall porter he knew, who was instructed to hire a cab and take Cloudsdale to a place where he might hide. Quite possibly the Bayswater apartment served this purpose. The journey there and back could be done in an hour. While the porter waited for Cloudsdale to appear, MacBrian had time to secure a fast hansom to Bayswater, where he lay in wait.

'If I am correct and Miss Noone was the lady with the yellow flowers in her hat, then Cloudsdale already knew her. She would have welcomed him and soothed his nerves. Perhaps she told him that she too was an innocent caught up in the schemes of others and had also been brought there to protect her.'

'Which of the porters was it?' I asked. 'I suppose Osmond must be the obvious suspect, as he was new to the post and could have been put there by the gang.'

'But which man would Cloudsdale trust the most?' asked Mycroft. 'I think the answer is plain. Drummond. He had been complaining of arthritis and was intending to retire before too long. Osmond was being trained to replace him. Drummond would have received a pension, but he would lose the apartment which came with his position. Maybe he was tempted by the prospect of a nest egg for his old age. I am sorry to have to point the finger at him, as he has been a loyal servant. Like Cloudsdale he might not have known what he was involved in. I cannot believe he knew the gang intended murder.'

'Also, it is too much of a coincidence that Drummond should have been taken ill at that time,' said Holmes. 'No-one could have predicted the sudden need to waylay Cloudsdale on his return to the office and had the time to give the porter something to ensure his absence from duty. Drummond feigned illness and Osmond had no reason to question it.'

'I agree,' said Mycroft. 'We have only Mrs Drummond's word that her husband was unwell and in the apartment for the full hour,' he added. 'She has her own duties to attend to, and he might only have told her he was there for that time. Naturally she would have supported her husband's story.'

The new evidence and our deliberations were notified to the police and Mr Ineson, and we were hopeful that Drummond, following his fall from grace, would be decent enough to confess and also exonerate Emmett from any involvement. It was not long before both porters and Mrs Drummond were in police custody and being closely questioned, an event which created shock and alarm at Whitehall.

The post-mortem report on the two corpses was complete, and the adjourned inquest was held before the Southwark coroner at the same session. In view of the manner in which the bodies had been stored it was not possible to arrive at the date of death, but it was generally believed that there being no sighting of either Cloudsdale or Collett on the days immediately following their disappearance, that they had died very soon after they had last been seen alive. Mrs Collett was granted her husband's death certificate and was able to claim the insurance money with which to pay for his burial.

The manner of death of the two men was very different. Collett had been killed by a single savage blow to the head, most probably with the crowbar presented in evidence. Cloudsdale, it was found, had consumed a drugged drink consisting of wine and a soporific. This had not been sufficient to kill him but bruising of the tissues around the mouth and nose suggested that he had been smothered.

Holmes remained of the opinion that Collett had been killed in the warehouse, while he believed that Cloudsdale was killed at a location where it was advisable that it should be done quietly without leaving signs of violence, either at the Bayswater apartment, or in a carriage taking him to Bermondsey. The jury had no difficulty in concluding that both men had been murdered but were not able to name their killers.

CHAPTER THIRTY-ONE

Weary from the burden of our enquiries, we knew that we were still far from a resolution. Holmes likened our task to attacking a solid mountain of suspicion and chipping away at it, bit by bit, but we were heartened by seeing some progress. Miss Jessup, we learned, had been vigorously working for her fiancé's freedom, calling on all his friends and associates to glean any shreds of hope, searching for small clues that might prove his innocence. When we paid a visit to Mrs Jessup to report our findings, her daughter was visiting Mrs Emmett. This was as well, in view of the questions Holmes wished to ask.

The Jessup family lived in a small grey house, part of a terrace of narrow properties, of a type known as 'two-up two-down' available for rent at a few shillings a week. On the ground floor was a general living room, with a kitchen at the back, and there were two bedrooms above.

Holmes, Mycroft, and I assembled at a table on which tea had been laid, and while the strain and anxiety showed on Mrs Jessup's face, she was bearing up well.

She told us that she had just taken tea up to her husband and made sure he was settled and content before we arrived. He was able to carry out his woodwork at a little bench that had been set up for him, but it placed a strain on his back, and he was obliged to rest in bed much of the time. Despite this, he remained in good spirits. She and her daughter shared the duty of looking after him. I detected no note that this was a burden on the household which it must have been; there was only affection and wifely duty.

She was cheered a little by what we had to tell her. 'But I fear,' she said, 'that even if it is found that dear Mr Emmett is innocent, there will always be a shadow on his life. I doubt that he will attain the advancement he had hoped for. Millie's love for him is undimmed. They will still marry, of course, that is without any doubt, but it will not be easy for them.'

'There is no expectation for the future?' asked Holmes. 'No anticipation of a legacy or the maturing of an investment which would make their situation more comfortable?'

'Nothing of that nature,' said Mrs Jessup, sadly. 'I have been asked that before. Mr Ineson wanted to know. He was all questions. Is Millie the beneficiary of a will, which promises to make her fortune? Was there an inheritance by which Mr Emmett stood in the way of another's prospects? Was someone jealous of a possible advancement in his position? I know nothing of these things and neither does his poor mother.'

'I am sorry to broach a difficult subject,' said Holmes cautiously, 'but in the interests of helping Mr Emmet's case —'

'Oh, please proceed,' she said warmly. 'I would tell you all I know no matter how much it might pain me, if by so doing I could help that young man and my dear daughter to find the happiness they deserve.'

'It has been suggested to me that someone is jealous of Mr Emmett's recent engagement, and is trying to discredit him, in order to court Miss Jessup,' said Holmes. 'Might that be possible? Does your daughter have other admirers? Have there been any in the past?'

Mrs Jessup smiled fondly. 'My daughter, as I am sure you will agree, even from so slight an acquaintance, is a delightful young lady, beautiful, accomplished, good-natured. I am sure, despite her lack of fortune, she might have had a dozen suitors if she had wished. But her loyalty and devotion to Mr Emmett are quite obvious to anyone who knows her.'

'How did they meet?'

'It was at a church bazaar, a sale of work. I was there, too, and Mr Emmett had come together with his mother. Millie was just sixteen, and in view of her youth, the friendship necessarily proceeded very carefully and always in company. Mr Emmett, while his interest was apparent, was reserved, respectful, almost bashful. I was very happy for their meetings to continue, and their engagement was everything I had wished for.'

'She has never been engaged before? Never had another attachment however innocent, however brief?'

'No, never,' declared Mrs Jessup firmly.

'Have any gentlemen sought her hand, asked you or her father for permission to court her, and been told that her heart had already been given?'

Mrs Jessup was more thoughtful. 'Not in such a formal manner. But there have been a number of gentlemen who have hinted to me that had she been unattached, they might have been inclined to court her.'

'Might I have their names?' asked Holmes, briskly. 'Start with the most recent ones. In the last year.'

Our hostess was surprised at this request but fetched paper, pen and ink and after some consideration, wrote three names. 'This one,' she said, pointing to the first, 'has, I believe, gone to America. And this gentleman —' she pointed to the second name — 'was married six months ago and is likely to be a father before long.'

'And the third one?' asked Holmes, examining the list. 'Dr James?'

'If that is his real name,' she said, 'which I doubt.'

'Why is that?'

Mrs Jessup refreshed the teacups as she considered what to say. 'It is not a pretty tale,' she said.

'All the more reason for it to interest me,' said Holmes.

She nodded understandingly. 'Millie and I met him one day while we were shopping. He was well-dressed, well-spoken in an educated way, courteous. He seemed very friendly, but there was something in the way he looked at Millie that troubled me. It is not unusual, as you might imagine, for Millie to receive glances of appreciation, of which she always appears to be quite unaware. Or maybe she pretends to be unaware. That seems the safest thing to do. But I had the impression that Millie had particularly drawn his eye. He struck up a conversation, and asked if we could assist him in selecting a gift for his sister. We obliged and he purchased a lace-edged handkerchief.'

'Was Miss Jessup wearing one of her flower creations at the time?' asked Holmes.

'Why yes, she often does. It was a little pin of spring blossoms. He complimented her on it. Gentlemen do not always notice such things.'

'Please continue,' said Holmes.

'When we had finished our shopping, he suggested he might show his gratitude by entertaining us to tea. As it so happened, we were due to take tea with my brother and his wife, so we declined, but then he became very insistent. He said he would like to make an appointment to meet us again. For all his good manners, there was something about him I did not like.'

'He was too pressing?' asked Holmes.

'Yes, he was. But that was not all. There are gentlemen, I am sure you have encountered them too, who try very hard to give a favourable impression so as to be well liked, but one senses that underneath it is something else, which one might not like if it became more obvious. They are making a deliberate effort to be likeable, when it ought to come naturally to them.'

'Did you learn anything about him? His occupation?'

'He gave his name as Dr James, and said he was an instructor at a college. He did not mention the name of the college or the subject of his instruction, which I thought strange. He was going to give us his card, but then made a great performance of searching his pockets and said it was very unfortunate, but he did not happen to have one with him. That was also suspicious. We bid him goodbye, and he said he hoped he would see us again. I told Millie we should have nothing to do with him.'

'I think your instincts were correct,' said Holmes.

'It comes of experience,' said Mrs Jessup. 'I can see how a young girl might be flattered by such attention, but I also have good reason to know that type. Some years ago, a neighbour's daughter was taken in by a man of that sort. He was respectable in appearance, polite and attentive. He made appointments to meet her in secret. They walked out together. He offered her marriage. It all happened very quickly. Far too quickly. He told her he was a single man, a gentleman of property. Of course he was neither. She later found to her distress that he was married with six children and had entertained a string of mistresses, all of whom he deserted when they demanded he keep his empty promises. It was nothing but an amusement to him. My neighbour was a good woman; she looked after her daughter and the child. But young girls need to be warned before they ruin their lives. I made sure to warn Millie.'

'How long ago was it that you encountered Dr James?'

'About six or seven months on the first occasion. I only spoke to him once again, after that. I happened to encounter him when I was out shopping, and he asked after Millie, and I said she was very well indeed. I made sure to say that I hoped she would soon be betrothed to her sweetheart, and he was a fine young man with a post at Whitehall and good prospects.'

'What did Dr James say to that?'

Mrs Jessup's fingertips trembled at the memory. She put her teacup down very suddenly. 'It was not what he said, it was his face. Quite terrible it was. I think that was when he showed me his true character. He went white, but then he recovered and smiled and said he wished her every happiness. But he was obviously displeased. And — I haven't mentioned this to Millie in case it upset her, but I have seen him since in the street a number of times, not far from here. I fear that he has been watching us and found out where we live. It is very unsettling. I suppose I hoped that once Millie was married and had her own place, he would cease to be a trouble.'

'Can you describe this man?'

'Yes, he is about thirty-five, or maybe a little older, and rather thin in the face. Clean shaven.'

'And his hair? Long or short?

'I'm not sure I noticed his hair, as he didn't remove his hat. He just tipped it for politeness but didn't remove it.'

'And you would know him at once if you saw him again?'

'I would, yes.'

'I think you are entirely correct in your judgement,' said Holmes. 'The man is a villain and needs to be stopped. He may be endangering other young ladies. If you see him again, preferably not when your daughter is present, would you be prepared to make an appointment to meet him at a tea shop? Then let me know the place and time, and I will be sure to be there. With a policeman.'

Mrs Jessup smiled at the plan and agreed to it at once. 'Do you think he is the man trying to incriminate Mr Emmett?'

'That is very possible, yes,' said Holmes. 'He does not like to be thwarted. Finding that your daughter was beyond his reach has only encouraged him to pursue her. But that is how we will trap him.'

'I think,' said Holmes to me later, 'our man is within our grasp. I am sorry to say that Mrs Jessup, with the laudable intention of establishing that her daughter was betrothed to a man of promise, provided Dr James with a valuable clue as to his identity. Once he knew that Miss Jessup's fiancé had a Whitehall post he was able to use his connections there to put a name to his rival and plan his disgrace.'

'You think this Dr James is part of MacBrian's gang?' I asked.

'He may, from his description, be MacBrian himself. If we can exploit his cruel obsession, then finally we will lay our hands on him and prove the motive which will exonerate and free Mr Emmett. But time is of the essence, I want to find him soon, before he can do more harm.'

'How might we find him? I am sure you must have a plan, Holmes.'

'I fear that MacBrian may prove to be a slippery fellow. He will not have left us a trail that is easy to follow. But we must make the attempt, guided by his weaknesses.'

'Do you think he has any?' I asked.

'Every man has his weakness,' said Holmes. 'MacBrian's may be the belief that he is cleverer than others and can delude or manipulate them at will. One error from him may be all I require.'

CHAPTER THIRTY-TWO

We were not at that time in pursuit of Miss Noone and John Clay. Discovering those reprobates in a city like London would be an immense task, and Holmes, while wishing them to be apprehended, was increasingly unsure whether doing so would assist Joshua Emmett. There was a risk that their arrest might even harm Emmett's case, as they would have no compunction in placing the blame for their actions on others. Holmes thought they were currently lying low, and time spent searching for them would be better employed elsewhere.

MacBrian, however, was a promising target. If we could lay our hands on him then Mr Lambourn, the lens grinder, would be able to identify him as the man who had hired his stockroom, making him a strong suspect in the conspiracy to copy Mr Cloudsdale's consignment of secret documents. If Mrs Jessup identified MacBrian as the persistent Dr James, then the motive to spread lies that would ruin Joshua Emmett would become apparent to any reasonable jury. There was a good chance that Emmett, with the defence of a skilled counsel, would be acquitted of all charges.

MacBrian, it was believed, must have some connection to a respectable photography business. There were, however, more than two hundred photographic artists listed in the London trade directories alone. The police were already making enquiries, but it was possible that MacBrian had been employed under another name, and all they had was a general description. Holmes, who liked to prove that he could outwit the police, decided to enter the fray, and approached the search from another direction.

The proliferation of the electric telegraph in recent years had led to a growth in the number of businesses devoted to the construction of electrical instruments, but there were still far fewer of them than photographers, which narrowed our search. There were about twenty in London, scattered across the capital, but Holmes decided to concentrate his efforts on locations which were convenient for Fenchurch Street and the lens-grinding workshop, of which there were five, and I accompanied him.

'MacBrian thinks he is ahead of us in his knowledge and may not realise that we have deduced his method of photography and employment of the Jablochkoff candle,' said Holmes. 'We will find him, not by the camera, but by the light of the arc lamp.'

In anticipation of encountering a desperate criminal, Holmes was carrying a walking cane. It was slender but deceptively strong with a weighted head that could, if he simply gripped the other end, become a club. While innocuous to the casual eye, he could transform it in an instant into a powerful weapon.

It did not take long for us to discover a business where an order had been placed for an electrical arc lamp of the Jablochkoff type. We were hoping to discover the address of the purchaser, but even Holmes's wily questioning could not extract that information. We were told it had been delivered to a photographer's studio, Mossop and Co., about half a mile away.

We walked there with some energy in our step, hoping we might find MacBrian, but the reception counter was manned by the owner, a middle-aged gentleman of mild appearance.

'Good afternoon,' said Holmes, politely. 'I was hoping you might be able to advise me. I am interested in purchasing or having manufactured for me, an instrument known as a Jablochkoff electrical candle. Do you by any chance have such an item?'

The man gazed at us over thick-lensed spectacles. 'There has been some interest in them recently,' he said. 'We neither deal in them nor employ them. There is an instrument maker not far from here. You might enquire there.' Predictably he gave us the name of the business we had just visited.

'Can you recommend that business?' asked Holmes. 'Have you ever ordered equipment from them?'

'Not personally, no, but a man who was employed here did so a month or two ago. A box was delivered here with that business's label attached. He must have ordered it himself, and he paid for it and took it away.'

'In that case I would like to speak to him, to see if he would recommend the maker.'

At that moment we heard voices from behind a door at the back of the shop, both male and female. If that was the studio, could it be MacBrian at work, I wondered. Might he be within our reach at last? For once, I was more excited than afraid. Having Sherlock Holmes standing beside you with a club in his hand and a determined expression is a great allayer of fear.

'He is no longer here,' said the owner. 'In fact, he resigned his position soon afterwards, saying he had a better one. Magraw, his name was. I was sorry to see him go. He did the development and printing work here and was very efficient. I rather thought he was planning to start his own business, as a possible rival to this one, and did not like to admit it.'

'And where might I find Mr Magraw?' asked Holmes.

'I don't know. He did not leave a forwarding address.'

There was movement from the back of the shop. A lady and gentleman dressed in their most cheerful clothes, with expressions to match, emerged from the photography studio, thanking the man who had officiated. They paid for the sitting at the counter and were told when the prints might be ready.

'Hawkins,' said the manager to the young photographer, a tall fellow with hair so smooth and black it looked dyed. 'You don't happen to know where Magraw is nowadays?'

'I am sorry, Mr Mossop, I have not seen him since he left.' The photographer returned to the studio, and we heard from within the sound of voices, furniture being arranged, and the rattle of an exposed plate enclosed in its protective frame being extracted for processing in the dark room.

'How unfortunate!' said Holmes. 'Perhaps I shall visit some other studios in the vicinity and see if he is there. How shall I know him?'

'He is a thin fellow, long hair, aged about thirty or forty. If you do find him, could you let me know where he is now? Not that I distrust him, but it is always well to study the methods of someone who once worked for you.'

'I will be sure to do so,' said Holmes, with a conspiratorial smile to suggest that he knew what Mossop meant, and shared his interests. He supplied his card. 'And if you should happen to see him and learn where he now works, I would be grateful if you could send me a note.'

'Every man leaves a trail,' said Holmes, as we left the shop. 'The places he goes, the transport he takes, the things he purchases, the people to whom he speaks. It is like a thread, invisible to the human eye, and yet it exists. And we must find the means to follow it.' I could see that Holmes, hopeful of a quick result, was frustrated by this new obstacle to his progress.

'If I was MacBrian, I would know that the police were looking for me under that name,' I said. 'But if he is calling himself Magraw, he won't yet know that you have uncovered that name. That does give us an advantage.'

'Yes,' said Holmes, thoughtfully. 'Unless…'

'Unless?'

'Unless one of the men at the shop we have just visited, and there must have been three, judging from the voices I heard — Mossop, Hawkins and one other — knows something, and will go to warn him.'

Holmes abruptly darted into an alleyway beside the shop, beckoning me to follow. 'Let us wait and watch,' he said.

About ten minutes later a young man with light hair, whom we had not seen previously, left the shop. He quickly looked about him before hurrying away. 'And now,' said Holmes triumphantly, 'we have a trail that we can see.'

CHAPTER THIRTY-THREE

The art of following someone without being noticed is harder than it might appear. I once tried to follow Holmes on one of his enquiries, without success, as he probably saw more of my movements than I did of his. I still think of that episode with embarrassment. One cannot lose sight of the quarry but at the same time they must not become aware that they are being followed. A crowded street is both a help and a hindrance in that respect. Holmes's height did assist him in one way, as he was able to see further than most, over the heads of others in the street, but at the same time it made him more noticeable, more memorable. I watched him carefully and tried as far as I could to match his pace. I saw that he was careful to maintain as far as possible an even stride so as not to make any abrupt movements that might catch the eye and attract attention.

The youth we now followed was walking quickly, resisting the urge to break into a run. Fortunately, he did not have far to go, but mounted the front steps of what looked like a lodging house. He rang the bell and was admitted. We waited to see who would emerge, but it was only the young assistant, who hurried back in the direction of the studio, passing us as we paused to study the display in a tobacconist's shop window.

'What should we do now?' I asked.

'We wait,' replied Holmes. 'If MacBrian appears soon, we follow him, but I think he will be making plans to move on and conceal any evidence. He doesn't know he has been tracked to his lair. He thinks he has time.'

Holmes looked at his watch. 'He is not, I think, a man to panic easily; I expect he is packing his possessions. Stamford, make a note of the address and send a telegram to Scotland Yard. We passed a post office on the way. I will wait here. If MacBrian does try to escape before they arrive, I will have to deal with him myself.'

Holmes had judged his man correctly. I sent the telegram and when I returned Holmes was still waiting outside the house. MacBrian had not emerged. After a while, a detective joined us, having summoned two burly constables on the way, and we briefed them on the situation. We were not permitted to enter the house, but the policemen did, and it was most satisfying when they came out with MacBrian in custody. At Holmes's bidding I had gone to fetch Mr Lambourn of the lens-grinding business and he had no hesitation in identifying the prisoner as the man who had hired his storeroom. MacBrian said nothing as he was taken away to be charged, he only pressed his lips firmly together and smiled.

'We had better question his young friend before he finds out that we have MacBrian,' said the detective. 'Show me to the shop.'

At this, Holmes's eyes lit up. 'Of course!' he exclaimed. 'I ought to have thought of it. I have never laid eyes on the fellow, but the young man we saw could well have been John Clay. Now that MacBrian is in custody, he may re-think his position. I have one last chance to urge him to tell the truth.' Holmes dashed away and I followed him.

Back at Mossop's photographic studio all was quiet. The manager was at the counter, and there was no noticeable movement inside. The detective entered the shop, but Holmes plunged into the narrow alley adjoining it, which he must have suspected led to a rear exit. MacBrian's confederate would not yet have heard of his master's arrest, but if he was alert, he must have realised that if questions were being asked at the shop, then he would be obliged to take his leave. The arrival of a detective was stimulus enough for him to act. Moments later we saw him emerge from the back of the shop, with a satchel slung over his shoulder. He made for the street but stopped in the alleyway when he saw Holmes and me standing side by side, blocking his escape.

'John Clay?' said Holmes. 'I assume that is your name? I am told you are of royal descent.'

'That is true,' said Clay, unable to resist raising his head proudly. 'Now stand aside and let me pass!'

'Before I do,' said Holmes, with a bow, 'I beg you to be honourable according to your blood. Do not, I implore you, let an innocent man suffer. Joshua Emmett has committed no crime but is nevertheless about to stand trial. Your word, the word of a nobleman, may free him.'

Clay laughed. 'You do not know what you ask! That I shall never do!'

Holmes took a step forward, but Clay delved into his pocket and drew out a small bottle. It had a glass stopper which he pulled out. 'Do not come any closer or I will use this!' he said. I could not see what was in the bottle, but I know that anything requiring a glass stopper and not a cork ought to be treated with caution. He brandished it at us, and I had no wish to take any chances. Clay, however, had reckoned without the speed of Holmes as a swordsman and master of singlestick.

Holmes had dropped one arm to his side, and allowed his cane to slide through his hand so he was holding it at the point. Fast as a whip he lashed out. The gnarled end caught Clay hard on the back of his hand, and he cried out, dropping the bottle which fell to the ground and broke, spilling its contents. The only damage was to Clay, as the impact caused a few drops to escape the neck of the bottle and splash his forehead. He cried out and clutched his hand to his face. At that moment, the detective, who had learned that one of the employees had left the shop, emerged from the back door.

'This is John Clay, who is a wanted man, and an associate of MacBrian,' said Holmes. The howling reprobate was swiftly handcuffed.

Mr Ineson, when we next met with him, confessed that he was amazed by Holmes's success. 'I had feared that Mr MacBrian or whatever he chooses to call himself, would be a hard man to trace, but you have proved to be more than his equal,' he said. 'If you should ever decide to take up the calling of a detective, you have an accumulation of skills and knowledge far in excess of what is generally thought to be adequate for that profession. I would definitely employ you.'

Holmes merely inclined his head in polite acknowledgement. 'Has MacBrian confessed?' he asked.

'Thus far MacBrian's mouth is closed like the proverbial oyster,' said Ineson. 'He has been charged with a number of offences and has done nothing to absolve himself or even appoint a solicitor to act for him. I have the impression that he is waiting for something, a man to appear and either do all that is needful for his defence or even spirit him away. We know nothing of his family, his forebears, his origins. His real name, the place and date of his birth, are a mystery. He makes things hard for himself and also for the law. At present he is held for the copying and sale of government papers, and conspiracy to murder both Cloudsdale and Collett. Whatever happens, he is facing a long prison term and possibly even the noose.'

'Perhaps some time spent in the cells alone with his conscience will move him to speak,' I said.

'As to a conscience, I am not sure that he has one,' said Ineson. 'He may say something after meeting with an advisor who will make it plain to him how best to save his neck. We must be patient. Clay has yet to speak, but I think he will. Sir Crawford Yates must even now be shaking in his shoes. Other associates may still be found. We will learn more from them as they scramble to tell their stories and divert blame from themselves.'

'What of the hall porter and his deputy? Have either of them confessed?' I asked.

'Mr Drummond has admitted his involvement and is under arrest, but he seems to be a small wheel in a large machine and knows very little. Mrs Drummond, who of course is precluded from giving evidence against her husband, and young Osmond, are not suspected, and have been freed.'

'Has Mrs Jessup been able to identify MacBrian as the man who pressed unwanted attentions on her daughter?' asked Holmes. 'He was calling himself Dr James.'

'I had the opportunity of speaking to Mrs Jessup and also Scotland Yard,' said Ineson. 'Mrs Jessup was very heartened to learn that the mysterious Dr James had been apprehended and hurried to make the identification. However, she was unable to do so. In fact, she was adamant that MacBrian was not the man, who she said was much thinner about the face with sharper features. She was able to describe him to an artist who has made a drawing, which she has approved. It appears that Dr James is still at large.'

'And continuing to endanger innocent young ladies,' I said.

'Indeed. The police are looking out for him but that is all they can do. There have been some recent cases of unscrupulous men, some of them married to unsuspecting wives, who make it a kind of sport to importune susceptible women with promises of marriage and ruin them. None of them resemble the portrait of Dr James.'

This news was a devastating blow to our hopes of a new and powerful defence strategy for Joshua Emmett.

CHAPTER THIRTY-FOUR

A few days later we learned that a young woman had appeared at the lodging house at 25 Cranfield Terrace, Bayswater. Mrs Purdue recognised her as Mary-Ann, the maid formerly employed by Miss Noone, the occupant of apartment two. The tenancy period had come to an end, and the maid informed Mrs Purdue that she had come to collect her mistress's few belongings that remained on the property and hold them for her against her return. Mrs Purdue was obliged to inform her of the police visits, and the fact that the trunk and its contents were now at Paddington police station. The maid accordingly went to the police to tell what she knew.

Inspector Keating came to tell us about the maid's statement.

Miss Noone, she had said, was a lady of great charm and elegance. While employed by her during the last three months, she had become aware that Miss Noone had secrets, but it was not her place to learn more, only to do as she was instructed. Once Miss Noone had realised that her maid could be trusted, she had revealed that she was a secret agent employed to take messages, pass information, and arrange clandestine meetings. To identify herself she often wore a hat decorated with a spray of yellow silk flowers. The maid said she did not know who Miss Noone's employers were but had assumed she worked for the government and was not involved in any activity which was against the law. Miss Noone was a very kind employer and allowed her generous half-day holidays. In the first week of October, Miss Noone had gone away taking her luggage, and the maid thought she must be abroad, but had not been told when her mistress might return. She believed that Miss Noone was in fear of her life as she thought she was being followed by men intent on abducting and murdering her. She herself had no secrets and had told all that she knew. She had no knowledge of any meetings or visitors at the apartment.

'I am quite sure,' said Inspector Keating, 'that the maid knew more than she was saying, but I had no evidence on which to bring any charges or hold her in custody. I was obliged to permit her to leave, with the instruction that if Miss Noone was to reappear, she was to inform me at once.'

'I very much doubt that Miss Noone, or Miss No-one as she might be called, will ever be seen again,' said Holmes, 'for the very good reason that she does not exist. She and the maid are most probably one and the same person.'

Keating looked taken aback. 'I will note your suspicions, but without anything further there is really nothing more I can do. If I was ever to learn of her again in connection with a crime, it might be a different matter.'

'I have her in my sights,' said Holmes. 'The time will come. I believe that she was directly involved in the murder of Mr Cloudsdale. The method of his death suggests to me that part at least of the crime took place in the Bayswater apartment. He would have been at his ease since it was represented to him as a safe hiding place. And the mythical Miss Noone was there, someone he already knew, who could reassure him that all would be well, and he and his family would be protected. He was given a drugged drink and then smothered, either there or possibly in a carriage taking him to Bermondsey.'

'She could not have done that alone.'

'No, I think she and MacBrian were working together. John Clay might also have played a part if he had returned from Stepney. Then Cloudsdale's body was packed into a trunk and taken to Mr Roberts's warehouse. It was Miss Noone who initially drew him into the trap, wearing the hat with the yellow flowers. She must have told him that she was an agent for the government. I am sure she was able to appeal to his nobler sentiments. And maybe a man of his years could not help but be affected by the earnest pleas of an attractive young lady.'

With the date fixed for the opening of Joshua Emmett's trial in a few weeks' time, there was still some uncertainty as to his possible fate. The only comfort Mr Ineson could offer us was that the tea shop manager, Mr Bradley, who claimed to have seen Emmett and the lady with the yellow flowers in her hat walking in the park, would prove to be a poor witness whose recently improved financial situation would open him to suspicion of perjury.

There followed some bad news. John Clay, who now had a scar on his forehead which he would wear for the rest of his life, had decided to make a statement to the police. He said he was employed as an assistant to a photographer, Mr Mossop, and was learning the trade, which was an honest one. There he had met the other prisoner, who he knew as Magraw, who had asked him to help with his experiments in the art of photography. He freely admitted that he had taken a train to Stepney, the purpose of which was to purchase some materials for Magraw. While there, he had seen Mr Cloudsdale stumble on the pavement, which was wet and slippery after a recent shower of rain, and almost fall under a carriage, and had tried to save him. If someone thought Mr Cloudsdale had been pushed, they were mistaken.

He recalled Magraw telling him about a gentleman called Emmett who was due to attend a meeting in Bayswater and required someone to take the part of usher. He was engaged to be a valet for that meeting and admit the other gentlemen. He remembered Emmett arriving and after that there were several others in attendance. He did not know their names, but Magraw was not one of them. He was prepared to give evidence at the trial to that effect.

CHAPTER THIRTY-FIVE

Holmes and I were to meet with Mycroft at his club once more to exchange the results of our enquiries, but to our surprise he did not appear. It was extremely unusual for Mycroft to be late for an appointment. Even in the days before Watson knew him, he was most comfortable with a schedule that was very strictly established and adhered to. It was said that his arrival at the office was more reliable as to time than any watch. As we waited and checked our timepieces and the minutes ticked away, we became anxious that illness, accident, or emergency had caused his absence. We made enquiries with one of the attendants and discovered that he had not come to his club at all after work that day. We were about to go to Mycroft's lodgings to see if he was there when we were told that Sergeant Lestrade had just arrived and was waiting for us in the entrance hall. Fearing the worst, we hurried downstairs to see him. The policeman's serious expression did not bode well.

'Lestrade!' exclaimed Holmes. 'We had an appointment to see my brother today, but he is not here. Is he well?'

'Yes,' said Lestrade, 'he is well, and extremely busy; he has gone to see his friends. But I have heavy news to impart. Mr Mycroft told me you would be here and asked me to come and see you.' The porter indicated that we could use the meeting room and we retired there to talk.

Lestrade drew a deep breath as he seated himself. 'I am sorry to have to inform you that Joshua Emmett is dead. He was found in his cell this morning. A post-mortem is being carried out, but it appears that he tore his bedsheets into strips and hanged himself. I will know more when the surgeon has made his report.'

For a while Holmes and I were silent as we grappled with the shocking news. I am sure that we were both thinking the same thing. Neither of us had known Emmett for long but his friendship had meant a great deal to Mycroft, and the blow to him, the Emmett family and the Jessups would be an appalling loss to bear.

'Who discovered the body?' asked Holmes at last.

'One of the prison orderlies. We have yet to ascertain a time of death.'

'Is there any doubt that he took his own life?'

'He left a letter,' said Lestrade. 'His made his intentions and motivation clear, and he also included a confession to his crimes. I have shown the letter to Mrs Emmett and compared it with recent examples of his writing. The hand is undoubtedly his.'

'Miss Jessup —' I began. My voice choked in my throat, and I could not go on.

'As you can imagine,' said Lestrade, 'she is prostrate with grief. Her mother is attending her, and Mr Mycroft has offered to arrange for a nurse to be on hand if required.' He took a document from his pocket. 'I had someone copy the letter out, as I thought you would want to see for yourselves what it said.'

Holmes took the paper and laid it out on the table before us.

The letter was headed simply 'Newgate' and dated that day. One could imagine Emmett, who was being held at that gloomy prison on remand, occupying his daylight hours composing his final thoughts.

My dearest mother, my darling Millie, you are all the world to me, and I have resolved not to add further pain to the ordeal you are now suffering. The end I have chosen for myself will be brief, and what I suffer will be as nothing to what I have inflicted on others. You will never see me in the dock while my confession is read to the court or hear me condemned to spend the remainder of my life in prison. I am guilty of all the charges against me, but I will not submit you, the innocent, whom I have cruelly betrayed, to years of misery and shame. I cannot bear to think of those I love enduring a fate as long and unhappy as my own.

I like to imagine that my motives were good. I saw a means to shorten the long wait for the wedding we all desired. Before me was new hope, I pictured the sun rising on the first day of marriage, the years of tender joy that lay ahead. It was in that spirit that I allowed myself to make associates who promised me the world. I was not the only one to be deceived. There are those — and I will not name them — who were taken in by the same promises. My greatest crime has been not to tell the truth, but now, in my final hours, I must.

Please forgive me, as I am sure that He who must ultimately judge me, will do,

Jos

'This is an exact copy?' asked Holmes.

'Yes, word for word.'

'Has Mycroft seen it?'

'Yes. He says it is characteristic of Emmett to put others before himself.'

'And Miss Jessup?'

Lestrade shook his head. 'Not yet.'

'I think,' said Holmes, 'I should like to examine the original of this letter if that is possible. And I must speak to Mrs Jessup if she would permit me. Can that be arranged?'

'I will see what can be done,' said Lestrade. 'Was there any particular point you had in mind?'

'You recall our visit to the apartment in Bayswater when we examined the contents of Miss Noone's trunk and the items we discovered there?'

'Yes, of course.'

'I am interested in the item we did not discover.'

CHAPTER THIRTY-SIX

By next morning Lestrade had made the necessary arrangements, and we accompanied him to the home of Mr and Mrs Jessup and their daughter. The sergeant carried a stout leather writing case, with the precious last letter of Joshua Emmett.

'Oh, Mr Holmes!' exclaimed Mrs Jessup as we arrived. 'I am so very grateful to your brother who has been a pillar of help all through this terrible ordeal! He has sent a nurse who is even now seeing to my husband, and I really could not have managed without.' Her eyes were red and she clutched a handkerchief.

'How is Miss Jessup?' asked Holmes.

'I am sorry to say my poor girl has locked herself in her room and will not come out. I hear her weeping and wailing almost without ceasing. I am so afraid for her. I have tried to persuade her to come out, but so far, she will not. I don't know what to do for the best.'

'Has she seen the letter Mr Emmett left?'

'No, but she knows of it, and refuses to believe he wrote it. From what I could see the writing is the same. My poor girl has so many love notes. I compared it with the one which he sent for her birthday with a gift and can see no difference.'

'May I see it?' asked Holmes.

'Yes, of course.' Mrs Jessup fetched the gift which was a pretty little china vase decorated with swirls of colourful flowers. It was accompanied by a card which read: *'My dearest Millie, my darling wife-to-be, a birthday gift from your ever adoring Jos.'*

Holmes nodded to Lestrade, who opened the writing case and extracted the letter which he placed on the table. Holmes placed the little card beside it and took out his glass. He studied the two items carefully.

'Do you think the letter was written by Emmett?' I asked.

'The writing certainly appears to be the same,' said Holmes. 'And it is written fluently, without the hesitation of a forger making a careful copy. The signature is the same. He uses the contraction Jos, on both.'

'Yes, he always signed himself that way,' said Mrs Jessup.

'You have other notes in his hand?'

'Yes, Millie has them in a casket beside her bed.'

'Any that I might see? There is one detail I have observed, but without examining more examples I cannot be sure if it is important.'

'There are some she carries with her — in her reticule. I will fetch them.'

More of the little notes were brought and laid out on the table.

Holmes spent some time hunched over, examining the writing, during which Lestrade, Mrs Jessup and I did not dare address him. At last, he straightened his back and nodded. 'The prison letter is a forgery. In a letter of this kind one must always make allowances, there will be small differences to the writer's usual hand, produced by emotion. The forger has made an excellent copy, but while the words express feeling, the hand does not. It does not tremble; the letters are performed with great exactness. It is an exercise in writing and tells me more about the character of the forger than it does about the man he purports to be.'

Lestrade stared at the letter again. 'I think I see what you mean,' he said. 'But that is not conclusive. Emmett might have been making the effort to control himself. And men often feel relieved when they finally make a confession of their guilt.'

'There is more,' said Holmes. 'I have compared the writing word by word and letter by letter and I see one difference. A significant difference. The forger must have known Miss Jessup's Christian name and how she was addressed in familiar fashion, but he did not know exactly how Mr Emmett wrote it. See here —' he pointed to one of the notes — 'and here again. The capital M as in "My". In normal use it is quite plain, but when he writes his fiancée's name, "Millie", he adds a little decoration, a final upstroke, a sweep of the pen like a flower. It exists everywhere except in the prison letter. The forgery is a highly expert piece of work. In fact, I only know of one man skilled enough to have accomplished it. He had for his guide a lengthy example of his subject's usual handwriting.'

'But there was nothing missing from Emmett's desk,' said Lestrade.

'No, and I am sure he would have noticed if anything had been taken. A copy would not do, the forger needed an original manuscript with all the little nuances of his subject's hand. What he received was the essay written by Emmett at the Bayswater apartment, the one item which was not amongst the things we found when we searched it. I do not think this confession was written by Joshua Emmett. I do not believe he took his own life. Joshua Emmett was murdered.'

Mrs Jessup gasped. 'Mr Holmes, do you think that news would persuade my poor girl to leave her room and take some refreshment? What you have said would not, I think, add to her grief, which could hardly be any greater than it is, but she would be better off knowing that Mr Emmett was innocent and did not make away with himself.'

'Perhaps you could speak to her,' said Holmes.

'Yes, I will do so.' Mrs Jessup sighed. 'My poor husband. I have not yet told him of our new tragedy. He was doing his woodcarving, and it brings him so much comfort, and now he rests. I will leave him a little longer.' She left us and hurried upstairs.

We waited and after a while the sobs and groans of the afflicted young woman were apparent, even from a distance and through the closed door, but when Mrs Jessup returned it was to report that her daughter still remained in her room.

'I wish I knew what to say to her,' said the distraught mother. 'I have begged her to come out and have a little food, but she will not.'

'Might I speak to her?' I asked.

'Yes, please do,' she said.

For once, Holmes did not suggest that this would be a task more suited to him than me. He could be charming and persuasive towards women, eliciting confidences from them before they knew it, but coaxing a distressed lady from behind a firmly closed door was outside his experience. I had had a little practice at this, admittedly with my cousin Lily following the abrupt ending of one of her engagements, but the one thing I did know was that it was impossible either through cajoling or inducements, to make her do anything she did not want to do.

I went to the bedroom door from which the sounds of distress were emanating, and knelt on the floor outside, to be more level with the keyhole. 'Miss Jessup,' I began, 'this is Arthur Stamford, Mr Holmes's friend.'

I heard a sniffle from within the room.

'Is there anything you require? You have only to name it and I will do my best to provide it for you.'

I waited, and after a while there was a curious gulping sound, and a whisper. 'Forgiveness.'

'For Mr Emmett? There is no need for that, as he is wholly innocent. We all know it now. The world will know it. Holmes will make sure of that.'

'For me,' she said. 'Who can forgive me?'

'We have all done things for which we seek forgiveness,' I said. 'But I cannot imagine what you might have done which would require it.'

She uttered a wail of pain. 'I can never be forgiven! I have killed him!'

'I don't understand,' I said.

'Joshua my only love. I killed him.' She dissolved into sobs.

I saw a familiar shadow, and found Holmes standing behind me, his face grim. He had a large chisel in his hand. 'This has gone on long enough,' he said.

CHAPTER THIRTY-SEVEN

It took very little time for Holmes to prise away the lock and fling open the door. The sight before us was something I will never forget. Miss Jessup was sitting on the floor, and for a moment I thought she was weeping tears of blood, which were running down her cheeks. My next thought was that she had destroyed her own eyes because there was blood caked on her fingertips. I ran to her and she shrank away from me, but I held her so I could see what she had done. It was not as bad as I had feared but even so, she had clawed deep gouges down her cheeks with both hands, and there was dried blood and skin under her fingernails. She had ruined her beauty as a form of penance for whatever sin she thought she had committed.

Mrs Jessup rushed in with Lestrade and screamed at the sight. For a moment I thought she would collapse into a faint, but the sergeant hurried to support her. 'Be strong!' he exclaimed. 'You are needed to help your daughter!' She gasped for breath but gathered her courage and did not fall.

I ordered her to bring a basin of water and clean towels and bandages, and encouraged by the need for action, she rushed away. I lifted the weak and afflicted young woman onto the bed and took her hands in mine so she could do no more damage to her face. 'Rest now,' I said. 'Rest and I will tend to you.' This seemed to calm her a little.

Holmes and Lestrade stood by and allowed me to do what was needed. When the water and other necessaries arrived, I cleaned the wounds and applied a salve, then dressed them as well as I could.

Mrs Jessup brought some warm broth, and the patient was able to take small spoonfuls of that nourishment, although it was with an effort. Gradually, the soothing influence of the kindness around her had its effect, and she lapsed into what must have been the first sleep she had had since receiving the tragic news. Her mother sat beside her, and I withdrew from the room together with Holmes and Lestrade.

'Why does she imagine she is responsible for Emmett's death?' I said to Holmes. 'She has done everything in her power to save him.'

'Has she?' said Holmes. 'I very much fear — but no, I will not speak it, it is too horrible for words. We must wait until she is able to tell her story.'

'I think her mind has been broken by grief,' said Lestrade. 'What she says is impossible. I will assume, unless I hear otherwise, that she never said such a thing. I only hope that rest and food and the love of her family will restore her. And Mr Holmes, I am grateful for your observations on the letter. I will compose a report and see if some good can come of it.'

Careful not to disturb the sleeper, we spoke softly to Mrs Jessup, making our farewells before we departed. Holmes added that when Miss Jessup was stronger and felt able to speak to him, he would be instantly available. He did, however, reassure the anguished mother that he was certain that her daughter was blameless.

When we next saw Mycroft the poor man appeared to have aged twenty years. He was only thirty, but his face was fallen and haggard, and the bruised look about his eyes spoke of ceaseless work and want of sleep and nourishment. He was close to physical and mental collapse but would not admit it. Holmes did all in his power to help his brother, but it was impossible to console him or ease his pain. Mycroft could only assuage his suffering and guilt by doing everything he could to support the two bereaved households. Another man might have sought oblivion from a bottle, but Mycroft dared not do so in case he was needed.

The next day we were summoned to see Miss Jessup. She was rested and calmer, and we found her in an armchair, wrapped about with blankets and propped up with cushions. I examined the dressings and was glad to see that the injuries were clean, and the process of healing had begun.

Mrs Jessup took me aside. 'Will there be scars?' she asked.

'I am afraid there will be, but with time they should fade,' I said.

Mrs Jessup wept a little. 'She was so very beautiful,' she said.

'She still is,' I said. 'May I talk to her?'

'I think so, yes, but please be gentle with your questions.'

I sat beside Miss Jessup and began by advising her that she was doing well, hoping that she would be encouraged to speak.

'Mr Stamford, I am so sorry I have caused such distress to my mother,' she whispered, her lips moving very softly. 'She is an angel. So good, so patient.'

I tried to reassure her that she took after that parent, but she shook her head. 'No. I have been foolish and brought misery to this household.' She glanced at Holmes, who was sitting nearby, and I half expected her to ask him to leave but she allowed him to remain.

There was a long silence before she spoke again. 'A week ago, I received a note. It was delivered to the house by a boy. I did not show it to my mother. It offered me the hope of saving Joshua and said that I should go to a bench in St James's Park at a certain time, where someone would meet me and tell me how this was to be achieved. It stipulated that I should tell noone else of the appointment. As it was a public place in daylight, I felt that it was safe to do as I was urged.'

I glanced at Holmes and his expression was severe, but he said nothing.

'I went to the place and sat down,' Miss Jessup continued. 'There were other people about, so I knew I could appeal to them for help if the worst should happen. I was almost expecting no-one to come, or perhaps a trickster demanding money, which of course we do not have. But after a few minutes a man sat down on the bench. I recognised him. It was the man we knew as Dr James.'

I felt a chill run down my spine, but said nothing which might dissuade her from continuing her account.

'He was very polite and asked after my health and that of my parents. He expressed deep sympathy for the terrible plight Joshua had found himself in and told me he thought the accusation was unjust. He then said that he could use his wealth and influence to gain Joshua his freedom, arrange for him to leave prison without a stain on his character, even help him advance in his career. He said he liked to assist worthy people who were without funds. He did not say what he would do to help, but he was certain of success. I told him we would not be able to repay his generosity, and he assured me that he would not ask us for a penny piece.' She took a deep breath. 'But there was a price. He expressed his admiration for me — I will not repeat his compliments — and how he wished most sincerely that we could be married. He asked me to break the betrothal to Joshua and be his wife.' She shook her head and tears ran freely from her eyes and blotted the bandages on her cheeks. 'I rejected him. I said I would never desert Joshua. I said that such a betrayal would be worse for Joshua than any prison, and as long as he lived, he would have all my love and devotion and loyalty, and I would never tire in my efforts to free him. And if he was to serve a prison sentence, I would wait for him as long as was necessary and marry him on his release.'

'What did Dr James say?' I asked.

'He said I should take a little time to consider his offer, and if I was willing to accept him then we should meet again at the same time and place in three days. I did not go to that meeting. But I never imagined what he might do. If he has influence enough to free Joshua, then he must also have the power to take revenge. On Joshua and upon me. Revenge for my rejection.'

'Miss Jessup,' said Holmes, earnestly. 'You must not blame yourself. This man, whoever he is, is a monster of evil. I do not think your rejection brought about the death of Mr Emmett. If you had agreed to marry Dr James, I fear that he would still have brought it about very soon after the knot was tied.'

'You think so?'

'I am sure of it.'

'I have been shown the letter supposed to have been written by Joshua in prison. Of course, he did not write it. I have treasured the little notes he sent me, pressed them to my heart, kissed them. Read them again and again, imagining his voice speaking the words. That letter was in the words of another man, a man who could not have met him.' She reached out impulsively and took our hands. 'Promise me something. Find the person who did this and bring him to justice.'

We made our solemn promises.

'Dr James had developed an obsession with Miss Jessup,' said Holmes when we next spoke privately. 'It began in the usual way, admiration for her youth and beauty and virtue. I assume he has had other encounters in which he succeeded in his vile ends. But Miss Jessup rejected him, and Dr James cannot abide rejection. He cannot tolerate opposition to his ambitions of any kind. What started simply as interest, in time became monomania. It was like a wound that would not heal and becomes poisoned and deadly. He became determined to have her and was willing to stop at nothing to achieve this. Had she succumbed to him, I have no doubt that he would have made her desperately unhappy, ill-treated her and then cast her aside.

'The one obstacle, as he saw it, was Joshua Emmett. He made use of his criminal plan — and I am convinced that he must be the author of the plot to copy and sell secret papers — to place Emmett under suspicion and destroy his reputation and prospects. But he found to his astonishment, that he could not shake Miss Jessup's belief. As the evidence accumulated, she stayed resolutely loyal. Emmett was arrested and committed for trial, and she was loyal; he had Emmett killed, but the false confession did not convince her for a moment, and still she was loyal.'

'Was it he who forged the letter?' I asked.

'Most probably a man as vicious and cold-blooded as he, whom he hired for the task. I have been wondering how the forger knew that Emmett referred to Miss Jessup affectionately as "Millie" and I think during Dr James's meetings with Miss Jessup and her mother he overheard that appellation. Naturally he would not have known how it was written. He also learned of her liking for silk flowers, which inspired him to suggest his spy should employ them. And now see what his machinations have driven Miss Jessup to do. I can only hope that he will not attempt to see her again. What a frustrated and embittered man he must be.'

It was Mycroft who stepped in to protect the Jessups, transporting them to a place of safety. Mindful of the machinations of the vindictive Dr James, he ensured that there were always eyes on their former home, in case the villain should appear in the vicinity, and could thereby be secured.

Holmes's work resulted in a re-examination of the case against Joshua Emmett and eventually there was an official announcement that the unfortunate clerk had been exonerated from all involvement in the crimes of which he had been accused. An editorial in *The Times* aroused a swell of public sympathy for Mrs Emmett and a charitable fund for her support was opened for subscription. *The Times* also paid tribute to the steadfast loyalty of the Jessups, who had never wavered in their belief that Emmett was innocent and whose efforts to free him had been fully vindicated. The editor reported that Miss Jessup had suffered the most and was a mere shadow of her former self.

Dr James made no further attempts to see Miss Jessup. His implacable nature was finally satisfied that by destroying her health he had exacted his full revenge on the young lady who had rejected him.

CHAPTER THIRTY-EIGHT

As the time drew near for the trial of MacBrian on charges of treason and the murder of Anthony Cloudsdale and Richard Collett, an air of pessimistic gloom settled over the Holmes brothers and me. Had we done enough to ensure a conviction on any of the charges? Would MacBrian, with the assistance of a competent defence counsel, be able to cast a mist of doubt over the prosecution's evidence? The prisoner had, so we were told, made the briefest of statements to the effect that all his actions had a perfectly innocent explanation. He appeared to be quietly confident that if he said nothing further, then no convincing evidence would appear to incriminate him. Counsel for the defence was, we noticed, one of the most celebrated and highest paid in the land.

As we took our places in court, MacBrian stepped into the dock with the air of a man who was already planning the celebratory dinner that would follow his acquittal. A strong waft of the tripe shop told us even before Mrs Collett made her appearance that she was in the courtroom. She said nothing, but positioned herself where she could stare at the accused, folded her brawny arms, and settled comfortably to watch. A number of persons who appeared to be tradespeople of Bermondsey, judging by their clothing and the fact that they nodded in a friendly fashion to Mrs Collett on arrival, occupied a row of seats in the courtroom. I hoped there would not be a disturbance, but they seemed orderly and peaceable enough.

The main exhibit carried into the court was the trunk in which the bodies had been found.

The opening statements of judge and counsel covered what for us was well-trodden ground; the disappearance of Anthony Cloudsdale, the copying of the secret papers he carried, his concern that he had been duped, the attempt on his life at Stepney and later disappearance, and the discovery of his corpse in a sealed trunk in a Bermondsey warehouse. There had followed the death and dismemberment of Collett and planting of the torso to divert attention from the search for Cloudsdale. The prosecution believed that the witnesses who would address the court would leave no room for any doubt of the prisoner's guilt.

The defence counsel delivered his opening address in a theatrical and confident manner. He was sure that when the jury had heard the evidence, of which he claimed there was very little, they would have no hesitation in acquitting his client, a respectable gentleman in the photographic business, of all charges. Much of what the prosecution brought before them they would dismiss as unreliable, and that which was believable, capable of a wholly innocent explanation. He sat down with a broad smile of satisfaction.

As each witness took the stand, however, an extraordinary and unexpected picture began to emerge. While it was impossible to demonstrate exactly what MacBrian had been doing behind drawn curtains at Fenchurch Street, it appeared that he had made something of a spectacle of himself in the Bermondsey area and left a trail of incriminating evidence. Mrs Collett testified to her husband's last day alive and said that she recognised the prisoner as a man she had seen in Bermondsey on that day. She was followed by a dealer in old furniture and luggage, who pointed out MacBrian as the man to whom he had sold the trunk displayed in court, which had then been clean and empty. A manufacturer testified that the prisoner had purchased from him some tarpaulins and a supply of gutta-percha. A carter said he had seen MacBrian, with the help of Collett, delivering the trunk, which was heavy enough to require two men to carry it, to Mr Roberts's warehouse.

Mr and Mrs Roberts brought their record book to prove when the trunk had been delivered, then briefly removed, and returned. It appeared that MacBrian, after carrying out these strenuous activities, had quenched his thirst in the public houses on Bermondsey Wall, and several drinkers testified that he had boasted — his tongue loosened by alcohol — that he knew how to hide a body where it would never be found. A dock labourer confirmed that he had been hired by MacBrian to place the trunk on a vessel bound for the high seas and dispose of it in deep water. If the police had arrived to examine it just one day later, it would have no longer been there.

The defence counsel, continuing to maintain his belief in his client with some difficulty, called only one witness. John Clay, looking like the noble sprig he claimed to be, testified that he had assisted MacBrian in a photography business which he believed to be wholly lawful. They made and processed photographic pictures as requested by their customers but took no part in acquiring the material itself. Mr Cloudsdale had been one such customer, but that was all he knew.

In an attempt to rebut the plethora of evidence from Bermondsey, the defence counsel in his final address, claimed that every member of the parade of prosecution witnesses was lying, and his client was prepared to name another man who was present in court but who he knew was the guilty party. At this last claim there was a murmur of scepticism amongst the onlookers, and mutters to the effect that if MacBrian knew who was guilty why had he not said so before? The defence, which had once looked so strong, now smacked of desperation.

As the jurymen retired to consider their verdict, Mrs Collett smiled to herself, took a package from her apron pocket, unwrapped it, releasing a cloud of vinegar fumes, and consumed the contents with obvious relish. I looked around for John Clay, but he had vanished. MacBrian was taken down to the cells and his defence counsel, with rather less confidence than he had displayed at the start of the trial, hurried to speak to him.

I wondered aloud what they could be saying, but Holmes merely read his newspaper while we waited. It was only an hour before MacBrian was brought back to the dock. He was acquitted of treason, and of the murder of Cloudsdale, but declared guilty of the murder of Collett. The judge commented that he had escaped a verdict of guilty on the first two charges only because of insufficient evidence, and not because there was any proof of innocence. He was sentenced to hang and bore the news stoically.

As we left the court, we saw Mrs Collett and the prosecution witnesses loitering outside in hearty conversation, before repairing to the nearest location which sold beer. 'Most of the witnesses were lying, of course,' said Holmes. 'But I have no doubt that MacBrian was guilty of that crime and worse, so I cannot complain of the result.'

'Most of them?' I said.

'Oh yes. I believe Mrs Roberts's record book was accurate, but for the rest, their evidence was nothing but a great deal of tripe.'

Sir Crawford Yates was no longer seen in Whitehall. He had been questioned in depth by the police and provided a full statement of the circumstances of Cloudsdale's interception, claiming that he had been misled by forged documents, which he had been ordered to destroy, into believing that he was following government orders. He thought that he was working on a genuine scientific development which would enhance security: a brief application of special light rays to an unopened envelope which would on its delivery reveal if the seal was intact. His rank and position gave him the benefit of any doubts and he escaped arrest, but his career was over, and he retired in comfort on a substantial pension. Men in his profession often write their memoirs, but it was rumoured that someone had had a quiet word with him suggesting that for the good of the country, this would in his case, be inadvisable.

Mycroft, who was already a somewhat reserved man, became from that time onwards almost a recluse. He was one of the founders of a new gentlemen's club, the Diogenes, designed for men of a similar mode of life, preferring quiet and solitude to the company of others. He retained his powers of observation and deduction but used them only as an intellectual exercise. He devoted his energies to his work and made great advances in his career.

He was true to the promise he had made to his friend Joshua Emmett to be as a loving brother to Miss Jessup. The care of both the ailing young woman and her invalid father was a burden which Mycroft was more than willing to shoulder.

In time Miss Jessup, her scars now healed to narrow lines, recovered her health sufficiently to enable a return to the work which she found peaceful and satisfying, the creation of silk flowers and corsages. The only thing she was never inclined to do was make yellow rosebuds.

Ten years later she married the owner of the fashion company, a kindly gentleman, a widower many years her senior, who assured her comfort and happiness, and extended his generosity to the care of her parents during their declining years. She became the mother of two children, and Mycroft Holmes was their doting godfather.

The events of 1877 dissuaded Mycroft from taking an active role in any of Holmes's investigations for many more years. The peaceful surroundings of the Diogenes Club and his happiness at seeing Miss Jessup well settled in life eventually enabled him to emerge a little from the shell he had built for himself. Mycroft and Holmes were closer than either of them would care to admit, and when Holmes needed an ally who would provide instant unquestioning support in his own personal affairs, his brother was his trusted man.

Holmes too, was changed. Even in the company of those who knew of the events of 1877 he remained reticent in referring to it, but I often sensed as he sat in quiet contemplation, apparently asleep, but far from it, that he was exploring the tragedy in his capacious mind. If he and Mycroft ever spoke of it to each other they did not do so in my presence.

Holmes refrained from undertaking any fresh enquiries in the dark days of that winter, but having entered the gloom as a youth of twenty-three, he became in the following spring a man of twenty-four. He was harder, more intense, quicker to crush any brief spark of emotion. In later years, as a consulting detective, he was rarely unsettled by disappointment or failure. He now knew that he was not infallible, but the death of a client before an enquiry was complete always brought back memories he could not shake.

Watson did once in his published memoirs allude to one element of the case — the unfortunate warehouseman of Italian descent, although I believe that Watson's spelling (or maybe it was the fault of the typesetter) was not quite accurate regarding the victim's true name. His mention ought to have read Rico Colletti of the club-foot, and his abominable wife.

An idea has crossed my mind regarding Mycroft, one in which I may be mistaken, but which has taken a hold of me and will not let go. Neither brother ever remarked upon it to me, and it was a subject which I could never, for obvious reasons, raise.

Mycroft loved.

It was a noble love, chaste and selfless, experienced in the full knowledge that the one he loved could never return that affection. Mycroft had sought to achieve his desired happiness by witnessing the union in blessed marriage of the lovely Miss Millicent Jessup and his old friend Joshua Emmett. It was an outcome that could now never happen. Did Mycroft ever harbour the secret fear that had he never attempted to help Emmett by joining forces with his brother to exonerate his friend from blame that the fate of the couple might have been different? I rather felt that nothing he or Holmes could have done would have changed anything, except that without them, the villains would never have been caught.

Many years have passed, and as I write this memoir, the lady I once knew as Miss Jessup lives quietly with her married daughter and grandchildren. She is surrounded by love. Those whom she has lost: her devoted husband, loving parents, her twin soul, Joshua Emmett, and dear friend Mycroft, who fell asleep for the last time at the Diogenes Club in his favourite armchair, all live on in her heart.

It was inevitable that Holmes would not remain satisfied with the apprehension and conviction of Drummond and MacBrian. He determined to capture and bring to justice all the members of this evil gang. He was able to identify the prison guard who he was sure had carried out the murder of Joshua Emmett, but before the man could be arrested, the villain fell victim in a quarrel with his own desperate associates and was killed in the most brutal manner. Holmes remained constantly on the alert for any news of the elusive and dangerous Miss Noone and the unrepentantly wicked John Clay. It was only some years later, once he had the full resources and commanding assurance of being a professional detective, that he eventually succeeded in bringing them both to justice.

One man remained at large, the worst of them all, he who had gone under the false name of Dr James and was the author of the tragedy. Wounded by rejection, he had become even more implacably vicious than before, but now he challenged society as a whole. For him, the ultimate satisfaction was the exercise of his mind in devising criminal schemes, in which he would triumph over the forces of the law.

Holmes has always believed that just as there are a few great detectives there are also master criminals who match them in skill, intelligence, and organisation. He sensed the genius that lay behind the Whitehall plot and other similar crimes that came to his attention, an individual who planned and directed events, but did not carry out the work himself. Such a man never soiled his hands, or even appeared where a crime was being committed. This was a true master of evil, who watched carefully for potential recruits, those with expertise, strong nerves, and heartless villainy, and drew them into his net. He was the spider at the centre of the web, spinning his silken threads; the puppet master who pulled the strings simply for the pleasure of control, and was capable of any wickedness to achieve his ends.

It was many years before Holmes was able to identify this adversary and put a name to him.

Moriarty.

HISTORICAL NOTES

Mycroft Holmes first appears in the canonical stories in 'The Greek Interpreter', one of the set of memoirs which ends with Holmes's supposed plunge from the Reichenbach Falls in 1891. To say that Conan Doyle was often uninformative about the dates of Holmes's adventures in his stories is something of an understatement, as Holmesian scholars will attest, and assigning a chronology to his cases can be a challenge. The story states only that it took place in the summer, and since Watson is living at Baker Street it is before his marriage to Mary Morstan, whom he met in September 1888, and most probably married the following spring. The summer of 1888 is therefore a likely date for Watson's first meeting with Mycroft.

Locations

The Paris catacombs, consecrated in 1786, houses the remains of millions of Parisians. From the early nineteenth century the site could be visited by appointment and was occasionally used as a novelty location for private entertainments. By the 1870s it was a popular attraction for the general public and remains so to this day.

Before its move to the Government Offices on Great George Street, the Treasury, where Mycroft would have worked, was housed in a building designed in 1734. Surviving bomb damage in 1940, it still stands on Horse Guards.

Stepney railway station was opened in 1840. It was renamed Stepney East in 1923 and Limehouse in 1987. It is currently Limehouse DLR. I have done my best to establish what lines and rail stations were open in 1877 and the timings of the trains. I apologise in advance for any errors, which do not, I believe, materially affect the story.

In 1888 Millbank mortuary was described as: 'in the yard attached to a dwelling-house and shop, and it is almost devoid of the proper modern appliances. A few wooden partitions have been run up, but there is neither sufficient room to conduct post-mortem examinations, nor means for ensuring the most ordinary sanitation and assisting in the ready and safe identification of the dead.' *Daily Telegraph*, under the heading 'The Whitehall Murder', 4 October 1888, p. 5.

I do not know when this makeshift mortuary was first brought into use. Newspaper reports reveal that there was no mortuary in the area in 1876, a situation much deplored by the coroner, but a body was taken there in June 1878. Directories and census returns show it was at number 33 Millbank Street and the keeper was Henry White who lived nearby.

The original Lambeth Bridge was opened in 1862. Although intended for use both by horse-drawn traffic and pedestrians, the unusually steep approach and concerns about its safety meant that it was soon used only by pedestrians. The current bridge was opened in 1932.

The mortuary in the churchyard at St Olave's, Tooley Street, was in use by 1876. The church fell out of use and was demolished in the 1920s.

Westminster Police Court as described here was built in 1846 and housed both the police station and the courts. The building was accessible from both Vincent Square and Rochester Row.

By the 1860s London's Docklands had become a centre of heavy industries of many kinds, such as the manufacture of ship's cables, telegraph cables, cement works and iron works.

Paddington police station was opened on the Harrow Road in March 1866.

Bermondsey Wall hostelries in 1877 were The Golden Fleece, The Grapes, The Three Mariners, Admiral Tyrell, and The Old Justice. There was a tarpaulin maker at number 23.

Technology

Electrical carbon arc lighting was first invented by Sir Humphry Davy in the early 1800s. In 1876 Russian engineer Pavel Nikolayevich Yablochkov (often rendered Jablochkoff), (1847–1894) introduced a major development. This enabled the carbon arc to be used as a practical system of lighting, since the power could be allocated to a number of small individual lamps, which became known as Jablochkoff candles. These were demonstrated in England in 1877 but the first commercial use was in the Marengo Hall, at the Grands Magasins in Paris that year.

Huge advances were made in the development of electrical generators in the 1860s and 1870s, when they started to be used for industrial purposes. Photographers who until then had had to rely on bright sunlight as the best source of illumination for their work, gas and candlelight not being suitable, saw the possibilities and began to experiment with the use of the new electrical carbon arc lamps. The press reports that the London Stereoscopic Society, which had a large corner outlet at 108–110 Regent Street, was using electricity as illumination for photography in 1878.

In the 1870s the Royal Navy was producing the first self-propelled torpedo, invented by English engineer Robert Whitehead (1823–1905) at the Royal Laboratories, Woolwich. The first steerable torpedo was devised by Irish-born engineer and inventor Louis Brennan (1852–1932) in 1874 and patented in 1877, at which time it was still under development. It was adopted by the British War Office for harbour defence in the 1880s.

The explosion of the experimental torpedo in the Baltic described in this book was suggested to me by a real incident, the tragic result of a torpedo test carried out by HMVS *Cerberus* on 5 March 1881.

People mentioned

Police Surgeon Thomas Bond (1841–1901) is best remembered nowadays for his detailed report on the Whitechapel murders of 1888. He was noted for making conclusions about murderers from an examination of the victims and is considered to be an early exponent of profiling.

Thomas Foinette (1835–1908) was Chief Inspector (later Superintendent) of Metropolitan Police B division, Westminster.

Edmund Humphrey Woolrych (1806–1883) was appointed a police magistrate in 1861 and sat as Metropolitan Police Magistrate at the Westminster Police Court until he retired in 1879.

Inspector James Keating (1844–1889) was stationed at Paddington police station.

Mr George Reader (1852–1922), a solicitor and Mr Edward T. E. Besley (1826–1901) a barrister, are both mentioned in the London press of the 1870s as presenting cases at the police courts.

Charles St Clare Bedford (1810–1900) served as the Westminster coroner for forty-five years.

Matthew Fox, born in Ireland in 1833, was Inspector of Police Southwark Division. He retired due to ill health in 1885.

Holmes finally caught up with John Clay in 'The Adventure of the Red-Headed League'. He never mentioned how Clay received the acid burn on his forehead and I have taken the liberty of offering an explanation.

In June 1889, Holmes was to plunge into the opium dens of the London wharves in 'The Adventure of the Man with the Twisted Lip'.

Readers of earlier books in this series should have no difficulty in guessing where Holmes had met the veiled lady before, and the identity of the master forger.

In 1877 Holmes was a novice in the art of burglary, but he had recognised its usefulness to a detective. Some years later as revealed in 'The Adventure of Charles Augustus Milverton', he was a highly accomplished burglar with his own complete and advanced set of tools. He initially refused to allow Watson to accompany him on that expedition. Perhaps the consequences of his earlier adventure with young Stamford weighed on his mind.

In 'The Musgrave Ritual', Holmes mentions some of his earlier cases, one of which Watson records as 'Ricoletti of the club-foot and his abominable wife'.

My thanks are due to M. J. Trow's *The Thames Torso Murders* (Pen & Sword Books, Barnsley, 2011).

For information about the provision of mortuaries in London in the 1870s I am indebted to 'Houses for the Dead: The Provision of Mortuaries in London, 1843–1889' by Pam Fisher (*The London Journal*, vol. 34 No. 1, March 2009, 1-15).

The City Hotel and British Mercantile Association are fictional.

A NOTE TO THE READER

The timeline of the events in the life of Sherlock Holmes in the canonical fifty-six stories and four novels has occupied, fascinated and sometimes frustrated Holmesian scholars for many years. The most commonly accepted year of Holmes's birth is 1854. He did not meet Dr Watson and occupy 221b Baker Street before 1881.

Almost nothing is known about his early life and very little about his education. I think it is possible that, like Conan Doyle, he spent a year at school on the continent, where he acquired his knowledge of modern languages. He is known to have spent two years at a collegiate university, which means either Oxford or Cambridge, although which one, and what courses he took have never been revealed, but he did not take a degree. The year in which he settled permanently in London is unspecified. His first recorded case is that of 'The Adventure of the *Gloria Scott*', as recounted to Dr Watson, which took place during the university vacation. Holmes had been developing his powers of observation and deduction and was known amongst fellow students for his singular method of analysing problems. At the time this was nothing more to him than an intellectual exercise. During his work on the *Gloria Scott* mystery, however, it was suggested to him that he would make a brilliant detective and that idea took hold and gave him a direction in life.

Holmes realised that he lacked the broad and varied fields of knowledge which would serve as a foundation for his mental skills. The next few years were dedicated to acquiring that knowledge, and in doing so, he created the man who burst upon the literary scene and met Dr Watson in the first Holmes novel, *A Study in Scarlet*.

In my work, I have suggested that Holmes was at university during the years 1873–75, solving the *Gloria Scott* mystery after his second year. Realising that his particular requirements could not be provided by a university course, he did not return, choosing instead to undertake his own studies. He had boxed and fenced at university and while there is no evidence that he devoted dedicated practice to either later on, it is clear that these were skills he retained. His lodgings in London's Montague Street placed him close to the British Museum where he must have spent many hours studying in the library, and he enrolled at St Bartholomew's Medical College for practical courses in chemistry and anatomy.

And that is where my series begins.

Reviews are so important to authors, and if you enjoyed this novel I would be grateful if you could spare a few minutes to post a review on **Amazon** and **Goodreads**. I love hearing from readers, and you can connect with me online, **on Facebook**, **Twitter**, and **Instagram**.

You can also stay up to date with all my news via **my website** and by signing up to **my newsletter**.

Linda Stratmann

2024

Sapere Books is an exciting new publisher of brilliant fiction and popular history.

To find out more about our latest releases and our monthly bargain books visit our website: **saperebooks.com**

www.ingramcontent.com/pod-product-compliance
Lightning Source LLC
Chambersburg PA
CBHW060424180626
46817CB00007B/2661